Legends of
The Mountain State 2

Legends
of the
Mountain State 2

More Ghostly Tales from the
State of West Virginia

Editor Michael Knost

Woodland Press, LLC

WOODLAND PRESS,LLC
Chapmanville, West Virginia

ISBN 978-0-9793236-4-5

For Mom and Dad.
You gave me excellent examples
to follow in life, love, marriage,
and parenthood.

"Hardboiled, Southern Gothic. I loved it. It's lean and mean and it doesn't care if you like it, which is what makes me like it all the better. Written with a razor on the back of a dead bloated redneck cracker down by the river side, the mountains in view, this is one excellent read."

— Joe R. Lansdale

TABLE of CONTENTS

Foreword
Gov. Joe Manchin III

As is often the case with West Virginia, it would seem our relatively small state packs a big punch when it comes to ghostly stories and folklore. In fact, West Virginia's history is rich in interesting backdrops for tales of supernatural creatures and various hauntings. It would seem that our ancient mountains hold many legends that are waiting to be shared.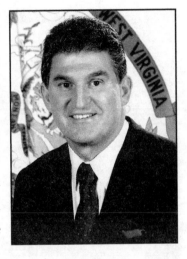

West Virginia is a beautiful state with a storied history that is ripe for tales of intrigue and, sometimes, spookiness and mystery. Mountain State culture has long employed the art of storytelling from one generation to the next, and in this way, many extraordinary and wonderfully eerie tales have survived.

When you read this book, you will find artfully written pieces wrought with ease and simplicity, which is truly the trademark of West Virginia. The stories included in this anthology are the fun kind that scared the socks off you around the campfire and will still make the hair on the back of your neck stand up today. The authors represented here have without a doubt mastered the misty genre of spooky narrative. Once you have read this book, I have no doubt you will be eager to share it with your family and friends.

Introduction
Michael Knost

After putting together this anthology's predecessor, *Legends of the Mountain State: Ghostly Tales from the State of West Virginia*, I realized we had barely scratched the surface with Mountain State folklore. Thirteen extraordinary authors contributed stories that left us goosebumped and scared of the dark. These writers did a fantastic job at painting tales around legendary ghosts and unexplainable events in the Mountain State.

After seeing great success with that project, the publisher asked me to put together a second edition—one that focused on thirteen additional ghosts and legends. Well, I knew there were certainly more legends to explore, but I wanted to ensure the new project would embody the same tone and texture of its forerunner.

In my opinion, the anthology you hold in your hands is a perfect continuance of the original project. *Legends of the Mountain State 2: More Ghostly Tales from the State of West Virginia* picks up where the first edition leaves off, offering fresh meat to those of us who devoured the original stories, which merely whet our appetites.

Enjoy your additional nightmares.

Dancing in Time to the Beating Heart of the World

Mark Justice

Mark Justice is the author of *Bone Songs, Deadneck Hootenanny,* and *Dead Earth: The Green Dawn* (with David T. Wilbanks). He also hosts *Pod of Horror,* www.horrorworld.org/poh.htm. Justice lives in Kentucky with his wife and cats, and infrequently blogs at http://markjustice.blogspot.com.

A week after I started at the hospital's pharmacy, I asked the janitor about the ghost.

"You ain't from here," Frankel said, as though that invalidated my question. The guy looked two hundred years old. I'd heard he'd been at RiverCare a long time. He had just finished mopping the basement floor as I was beginning my shift.

"No. I'm from Georgia. But I went to Marshall. I've been in Huntington almost six years now."

He stared at me as if he hadn't heard. He dropped the mop in the bucket and wheeled it away. Apparently Frankel didn't associate with the newbies.

I walked behind the counter and began my day of dispensing relief to the aged and depressed.

***

Another week passed before we spoke again. It was almost noon and my stomach was rumbling. I was on the phone with a drug rep. We were almost out of Lexapro and a couple other of the SSRI drugs, which around here was like McDonald's running out of Big Macs. After the rep assured me the shipment would arrive by close of business, I hung up. That's when I noticed old Frankel leaning against my counter.

"Her name is Angela," he said.

It took me a minute to process his words.

"The ghost? She has a name?"

He went silent again, and the way he looked at me made me realize he was waiting to see if I was going to make fun of him.

I rested my elbows on the counter. "Have you seen her?"

Frankel licked his lips and looked away. He smelled like stale cigarette smoke. RiverCare was a smoke-free facility, but I imagined Frankel had carved out a private smoking area in some dim closet here in the basement.

When Frankel finally looked up again, his eyes had a haunted quality. "Yep, I seen her."

A chill slithered down the back of my neck.

From my first year at Marshall I had heard about the ghost nurse, an apparition who walked the halls at RiverCare, which had once been a hospital for crippled children back when you could still call someone crippled. The stories had taken on new meaning to me two years ago when my fiancée had been killed in automobile accident back in Georgia. Paula was twenty. We had been together since freshmen year of high school. At the funeral, the words of friends and family were kind, yet underneath their solicitous comments was a message: You're young. You'll get over this. You'll find someone else.

Perhaps I would. But it didn't feel like it. Not today. Not for the past two years.

With Paula gone, the only thing left for me down south was the aunt who had raised me. I was happy to have escaped her, so I wouldn't be going back. West Virginia was my home now, for better or worse.

"Did . . . did you know her?" I said.

Frankel opened and closed his mouth. He quickly turned and left the pharmacy.

***

For the next few weeks Frankel seemed to be avoiding me.

I was the only pharmacist on staff. My days were full, leaving no time to search out the janitor for a heart-to-heart. While counting out pills or taking inventory, I found myself wondering what I would say to him when our paths inevitably crossed again.

Before Paula's death, I would have ridiculed reports of ghost sightings or any tale of the supernatural. But losing her felt like half of everything I was had been ripped away, leaving a raw, gaping wound that could never heal.

I turned to religion for a while. Eventually, I realized the church held no answers for me. Doxology and platitudes weren't enough. I needed proof that something existed beyond this life. If I knew I would see Paula again, I thought I could move on.

***

I came in early one Saturday to complete the inventory. I could have put it off until Monday but it wasn't as if I had anything else to do.

Frankel was in the lobby, guiding a wax stripper across the yellowed tile floor. I stood quietly until he saw me. When I didn't move away he shut off the stripper. We stared at each other for a while, until Frankel swallowed and looked down at his shoes.

"Tell me," I said. "Please."

***

We had coffee at a stained and battered table in RiverCare's small cafeteria. At that time on a weekend morning we had the place to ourselves. Frankel had been slow to begin, yet once he got going the words spilled out of him.

"I started here in '46. Right after I shipped back from the Pacific. It was a thriving place then. Crippled kids came from all over the state. Kentucky and Ohio, too. Poor things. Some of 'em were too messed up to live long. In terrible pain. But Angela could always make them feel better, least ways for a few minutes. She would dance or sing for 'em, and they couldn't help but smile."

"She sounds like a good person," I said. Frankel was so deep in the past that I don't think he heard me.

"All she ever wanted to do was help. Kids or grown-ups, it didn't matter. It was just lucky for them little ones that she ended up here. She had

3

such faith that those poor kids were gonna end up in a better place." He looked directly at me for the first time since we sat down. "You ever have faith like that?"

I shook my head.

"Me neither. Not then, anyway. We used to talk, me and her. She didn't act like I was beneath her just 'cause I scrubbed toilets. She was somethin', boy. As pretty as a sunrise. It was like she was all lit up from inside, glowin' with a light you could see a block away. Always found the good in everybody. Even me."

"What happened?"

Frankel coughed so hard his face turned red. He pulled a handkerchief from his back pocket and held it over his mouth. I briefly wondered if I needed to find the on-call doctor. It took Frankel a full minute before he could talk again. There were tears in his eyes, and as he put the handkerchief away I thought I saw bright specks of blood.

"Sorry," he said. "I'm comin' down with somethin'." He took in a ragged breath before he continued. "The director of the hospital back then was a rat named Humphries. He had an eye on Angela. She would have been just another notch on his bedpost. But she wouldn't give in to him, no matter how many times he tried. He caught her late one night in one of the rooms, and he tried to have his way with her, right there where those kids were sleeping. They struggled, and Anglea fell, cracking her head open. She died on the spot. By the time it happened, though, a couple of other nurses heard the noise and witnessed what happened, so Humphries couldn't wiggle out of it. He died in prison. It was too good for him, after what he . . . he. . ."

I put my arm on his wrist. It felt as fragile as a twig.

"I'm sorry," I said.

"I've seen her three times in all these years. Always when I'm alone. Always when I'm at my lowest."

My skin tingled as though the air was filled with static electricity.

"And she's not alone," Frankel said. "The kids are with her. All the ones who passed here. They're all healthy now. No sickness. No metal braces or crutches or tubes sticking in 'em. Anglea always smiles at me with that smile that could lift a thousand angels into the sky. She's still helping people. Even now."

4

A single tear rolled down his cheek.

I didn't say a word.

***

Two years passed and I didn't see or hear any sign of the ghost.

Frankel died six months after our conversation in the cafeteria. I was the only mourner at his funeral.

I started dating again. Marta was one of my drug reps. We'd shared a few classes at Marshall. I enjoyed her company, but memories of Paula were never far away. Marta eventually told me that I was too sad, that dating me was a full-time job. She said she needed more light in her life.

So I found myself alone again. It was a familiar place.

I'd started coming in early on Saturday mornings to catch up on work, mostly because I liked to keep busy, to steer my thoughts away from darker terrain.

I rarely saw anyone on those mornings. After Frankel died, the hospital contracted the cleaning to an outside company that worked late at night.

I was busier than ever; the hospital's patients weren't finding the golden years a party. Many of them were tired of living and scared of dying. Despite my relative youth, I felt like I was becoming one of them.

When the light flickered I was alone in the hallway in front of the pharmacy, fumbling with my keys and trying not to drop my coffee. I thought it was one of the overhead fluorescents dying.

Until the temperature suddenly dropped and I saw the white cloud of my own breath.

I turned, and saw a woman standing behind me, surrounded by a golden nimbus.

She was dressed in a nurse's uniform from sixty years ago, white and freshly pressed.

She was pretty, but it was her smile that elevated her to beautiful. It was warm and compassionate, without guile. I saw it and knew I could tell her anything. More importantly, I knew she would understand.

She was everything Frankel had said.

Seeing her was such a stunning experience that I wasn't aware of the children. There must have been a hundred of them. They filled the hallway behind Angela, and they skipped and danced and ran around, all of them smiling.

At the back of the hall, Frankel stood, holding hands with two of the children.

He was young, and he stood straight and tall, free of the infirmities of age and disease. He nodded to me.

Angela stepped forward. The pressure in my chest grew heavier.

She touched my face and all the pain, all the melancholia simply ceased. I felt new.

She stepped back, watching me.

I took a deep breath. The air tasted so clean.

Angela's smile grew wider. She gestured gracefully, guiding my gaze to another woman who stood behind her.

It was Paula, just as I remembered her: tall and athletic, her short hair and dark eyes both the color of coffee. She was dressed simply in jeans and a sweater.

I didn't know my legs had given out until I sat down hard on the floor.

Like Frankel, Paula held the hands of two children who stared up at her with adoration. Paula grinned at me, in that mischievous way I'd fallen in love with when I was 14.

Angela touched Paula's shoulder and nodded to me.

I understood. Paula was happy.

"Thank you," I said. My voice was a raw whisper.

That golden light dimmed, then faded completely. I saw Paula lift one of the kids, a small girl, into her arms. The girl hugged her neck as Paula winked at me.

Then I was alone in the hallway.

No. I wasn't alone. I felt the pulse of the earth. I was part of the world again.

Frankel was right. Angela was a healer. And she had given me back something I thought had been forever lost.

She had given me hope.

I sat in the floor for a long time. Eventually, I stood and went inside the pharmacy.

After a time, I picked up the phone and dialed Marta's number from memory.

It was time to join the dance again.

The Adventure
of the Greenbrier Ghost

Jonathan Maberry

Jonathan Maberry is a multiple Bram Stoker Award-winning author, magazine writer, playwright, and lecturer. He is co-creator and consulting producer for "On the Slab" (Disney/Stage 9). His books include *Ghost Road Blues*, *Dead Man's Song*, *Bad Moon Rising*, *Vampire Universe*, *The Cryptopedia*, *Zombie CSU*, and *Patient Zero*. Visit Jonathan on the Web at www.jonathanmaberry.com.

In late November of 1896 I had the pleasure of accompanying my good friend Mr. Sherlock Holmes on a cruise to America. Rather discretely, he had been approached by a representative of the American government to help with a matter concerning a suspected forgery of the Declaration of Independence. Although this was a very grave matter, and one that could easily have shaken the foundations of the young and mighty nation, it took Holmes less than a single afternoon to put the matter right and to hand over the notorious Canadian forger DesBarnes to the authorities.

It was all hushed up and I allude to it now only to establish that Holmes and I were indeed in America at the end of that year, and we decided to take the opportunity to enjoy a rail trip from Washington, D.C., throughout the southern states, which were enjoying fine weather despite the time of year.

Our plan was to return to Norfolk in Virginia in late February and from there take ship back to England. The weather and relaxation had done Holmes a world of good and he was more animated and less laconic than he had been in recent months. It did nothing but raise his spirits to discover that crime was rife in the American south—and indeed throughout much of this vast country. As states were being settled and industry introduced to all quarters there was as much room for corruption, treachery, theft, and mur-

7

der as there was for the more placid and commonplace pursuits of growth and settlement.

On the sixteenth day of February we found ourselves in the shipping office at Norfolk making arrangements for several large trunks of chemicals, specimens, and books to be shipped back to our lodgings at 221-B Baker Street when a young man in the livery of a telegraph employee came running toward across the wharf calling Holmes's name. The young fellow skidded to a stop, knuckled his cap and thrust out a message.

Holmes took it with a bemused expression. It was neither the first nor the tenth such urgent communiqué he had received during our journey. As he tipped the boy and unfolded the message I murmured, "Holmes, our ship sails with the dawn tide. We don't have time for any—"

He cut me off with this singular question, "Do you believe in ghosts, Watson?"

I hesitated, for Holmes had tricked me more than once with such a question only to trounce any credulity I had with some fact or scientific proof. "Many do," I said vaguely.

"You are getting careful in your dotage, Watson." There was mischief in his eyes as he handed me the note. "Read this and then decide if you want to catch our boat or wait for another tide."

I stepped into a patch of sunlight to read the letter, which was short and enigmatic.

Dear Mr. Holmes

My daughter was murdered. Her ghost has told me the name of her killer. For the love of God and justice please help.

Mrs. Mary Jane Robinson Heaster
Richlands, Greenbrier County, WV

I looked up and saw that Holmes was staring, not at me but at the shadows clustered under the eaves of the shipping office, his lips pursed, eyes narrowed to slits.

"Her daughter's ghost has revealed the identity of her killer?" I said

with half a laugh. "Surely this is the rant of a distressed and overly credu-
lous woman, Holmes. We've heard this sort of rubbish before."

"And yet, Watson," he said as he took back the letter, "and yet. . ."

Holmes left it hang there and turned on his heel and marched across
the shipping yard to the rail transport office. With a resigned sigh and weary
shake of my head I followed.

***

America is a railroad nation, perhaps as much as England, though its scope
is Olympian. We took three connecting trains and within two days we were
rattling down a country lane in a wagon pulled by a pair of brown horses.
The driver chewed tobacco and every few minutes would spit across to the
verge with great accuracy and velocity.

"Tell me, my good man," said Holmes, pitching his voice above the
rumble of the wheels, "do you know Mrs. Heaster very well?"

He turned and looked at us for a moment, chewing silently. "You
fellers are here about what happened to her daughter, aintcha?"

"Perhaps."

"Mrs. Heaster been saying that young Zona was kilt deliberate," said
the man, "but the doctor and the sheriff said it were an accident."

"And what do you think?" asked Holmes.

The man smiled. "I think it were all done too fast."

"What was?" I asked.

"The burial, that inquest, all of it. It were done fast like there was something to hide."

"Is it your belief that there was some mischief?" Holmes asked.

"Miss Zona were a country girl, you understand? 'Round here even
girls with breeding like Miss Zona grow up climbing trees and hiking them
hills." He made a face. "You can't tell me no country girl just up and tripped
down some steps and died."

"You don't believe that it was an accident?" Holmes prompted.

"I were born at night, sir, but it weren't last night." With that he spit another plug, turned around and drove the rest of the way in silence.

***

He deposited us at a lovely if rustic country house with a rail fence, chickens in the yard and a view of green hills. In London there would be a foot of snow but here in Greenbrier County it was like spring paradise.

Mrs. Mary Jane Heaster met us at her gate, and at once we could see that she was much troubled by recent events. She was a strong-featured woman, and her face was lined with grief. "Mr. Holmes," she cried, rushing to take his hand as he alit from the wagon. "God bless you for coming! Now I know my Zona will find justice."

I saw Holmes's face take on the reserve he often showed with effusive displays of emotion, particularly from women, and he took his hand back as quickly as good manners would allow. He introduced me.

"Heavens above, Doctor," she exclaimed. "I have read each of the wonderful accounts of your adventures with Mr. Holmes. My cousin is married to a London banker, and she sends me every issue of The Strand. You are a marvelous writer, Dr. Watson, and you make each detail of Mr. Holmes's brilliant cases come alive."

Holmes barely hid a smile that was halfway to a sneer. His opinion of my literary qualities was well known and he often berated me for favoring the excitement of the storytelling format instead of a straight scientific presentation of case facts. I'd long ago given up any hopes of explaining to him that the public would never read straight case reportage. I also thought it tactless to mention that many of our most interesting cases came about because of the notoriety Holmes had achieved with the publication of my stories.

"But I am a dreadful hostess," cried Mrs. Heaster, "making my guests stand chattering in the yard. Please come into the parlor."

When we were settled in comfortable chairs with teacups and saucers perched on our knees, Mrs. Heaster leaned forward, hands clasped together. "Can you help me, Mr. Holmes? Can you help me find justice so that my daughter can rest easy in her grave? For I tell you truly, my dear sirs, that she is not resting now. She walks abroad crying out for justice."

There was a heavy silence in the room and her words seemed to drift around us like spectres. Mrs. Heaster sat back, and in her eyes I could see that she was aware of how her own words must have sounded. "Of course, you gentlemen have no reason to believe such a tale. But I assure you it is the truth."

Holmes held up a finger. "I will be the judge of what is the truth," he said curtly. "Now, Mrs. Heaster I want you to tell us everything that has happened. Leave nothing out, however minor a detail it may seem to you. Be complete or we cannot hope to help you."

With that he set his teacup down, sank back in his chair, laced his long fingers together and closed his eyes. Mrs. Heaster glanced at me and I gave her an encouraging nod.

"My daughter was Elva Zona Heaster and she was born here in Greenbrier County in 1873. She was a good girl, Mr. Holmes. Bright and quick, good at letters and sewing. But—" and she faltered. "She got into trouble a few years ago. She had a child."

She let it hang there, expecting rebuke, but Holmes gave an irritated wave of his fingers. "I am a detective, madam, not a moral critic."

Mrs. Heaster cleared her throat and plunged ahead. "As you can appreciate, an unmarried woman with a child cannot expect much in the way of a good marriage. She resigned herself to living alone, but then in October of 1896 she met a man named Erasmus Stribbling Trout Shue. Most folks around these parts called him Edward, though I've always thought of him as Trout: cold and slippery. He was a drifter who came here to Greenbrier to work as a blacksmith, saying he wanted to start a new life. He alluded to a hard past but never gave any details. He went to work in the shop of James Crookshanks, which is located just off of the old Midland Trail. Trout had talent as a farrier, and in farm country there is considerable work for a man skilled at shoeing horses and cows. Shortly after Trout came to town my daughter met him when she went to arrange for shoes for our bull, which we let out to stud at local farms." Mrs. Heaster sighed. "It was love at first sight, Mr. Holmes. You've heard the expression sparks flew? Well, it was true enough when Zona went into the blacksmiths and saw Trout hammering away at his anvil. He is a very big and muscular man, powerful as you'd expect of a blacksmith, but handsome in his way. Perhaps more charming than handsome, if you take my meaning. He had a smile that could turn his hard face into that of a storybook prince, and the attention he lavished on Zona made her feel like a princess. He asked me for her hand in marriage and though I had my misgivings—it seems I am too old to be taken in by a handsome smile and thick biceps—I agreed. My daughter, after all, had such limited prospects."

"Of course," I said.

"From the outset I felt that Trout was hiding something, but he never let on and I found no evidence to confirm my suspicions. I began to think I was just becoming that proverbial old woman, yielding to fears and interfering with my daughter's happiness . . . but my fears were justified," she said, and as I watched I saw all the color drain from her face. "Worse than justified, for how could I know of the terrible events to come?"

Holmes opened his eyes and watched her like a cat.

"Zona and Trout lived together as man and wife for the next several months. Then, on January 23 of this year—on that terrible, terrible day, Andy Jones—a young colored boy who had been sent to their house by Trout on some contrived errand—came tearing into town, screaming that he had found my Zona lying dead at the foot of the stairs. He said that he saw her lying stretched out, with her feet together and one hand on her abdomen and the other lying next to her. Her head was turned slightly to one side. Her eyes were wide open and staring. Even though Andy is a small child he knew that she must be dead. Andy ran to town and told his mother and she summoned Dr. George Knapp, who is both our local doctor and coroner. Dr. Knapp was out at one of the more distant farms and it took him nearly an hour to arrive."

Mrs. Heaster took a breath to brace herself for the next part. "By the time Dr. Knapp arrived Trout had come home from Mr. Crookshanks's shop and he had taken Zona's body upstairs and laid her out on the bed. Normally, town women tend to the dead, washing them and dressing them for the funeral, but by the time Dr. Knapp had arrived, Trout had washed Zona and dressed her in her best dress, a long gown with a high collar, with a veil covering her face."

Holmes leaned forward. "Describe the veil and collar."

"It was a white veil recut from her wedding gown so she could wear it to church."

"And the collar?"

"Very high and stiff-necked."

Holmes pursed his lips and considered. "Pray continue," he said after a moment. "Tell me about the findings of Dr. Knapp's examination of your daughter."

"That's just it, Mr. Holmes, there wasn't much of an examination. Dr. Knapp tried, of course, but Trout clung to Zona throughout, wailing in grief and agony, abusing the doctor for disturbing his poor dear wife's remains."

"Were you there, Mrs. Heaster?" I asked.

"Yes, I stood in the doorway, shocked into silence by what had happened, feeling my heart break in my chest."

"Where was Trout Shue while the doctor was examining your daughter?"

"Excellent, Watson," Holmes said quietly.

"He sat at the top of the bed, cradling her head and sobbing," said Mrs. Heaster.

"Did he order Dr. Knapp to stop the examination?" Holmes asked.

"No, but he was so demonstrably overcome with grief the doctor relented out of pity and gave Zona's body only the most cursory of examinations. Barely enough to assure himself that she was in fact dead. However," she said slowly, "he did notice that there were bruises around Zona's throat."

"Bruises? What did he make of them?"

"Nothing, Mr. Holmes."

"Nothing?"

"Nothing."

After a moment's pause Holmes asked, "What did Dr. Knapp determine was the cause of your daughter's death?"

Mrs. Heaster sneered. "At first he called it an everlasting faint. I ask you!"

"That's preposterous," I cried. "All that says is that he had no idea of the cause of death."

"There was a lot of such criticism," agreed Mrs. Heaster, "and so when he filed his official report, Dr. Knapp changed it to 'female trouble', which shut every mouth in the county. No one will talk of such things." She made a face. "People are so old fashioned."

"Was there any history of gynecological distress?" I asked, but she shook her head.

"Nor were there any complications during the birth of her son. She was a healthy girl. Strong and fit."

I shot a covert glance at Holmes, who was as likely as anyone to steer well clear of such delicate matters, and indeed his face had a pinched quality, but his eyes sparkled with interest. "In your letter you allude to murder," he said.

"Murder it is, Mr. Holmes. Brutal murder of the boldest kind."

"And the murderer? You believe it to be Trout Shue?"

"I know it to be him!"

"How is it that you are so certain?"

"My daughter told me." She said it without the slightest pause.

"Your . . . dead daughter?"

"Yes, Mr. Holmes. For several nights she has come to me in dreams and told me that Trout Shue murdered her. She is caught between worlds, trapped and bound here to this world because of the evil that was done to her. Until justice is served upon her killer, my daughter will wander the earth as a ghost. That, gentlemen, is why I implore you to help me with this matter."

Holmes sat still and studied Mrs. Heaster's face, looking—as indeed I looked—for the spark of madness or the dodgy eye-shift of guile—and he, like I, saw none. She was composed, clear and compelling, which neither of us had expected considering the wild nature of her telegram. Holmes sat back and steepled his fingers. The long seconds of his silent deliberation were counted out by an ornately carved grandfather clock and it was not until an entire legion of seconds lay spent upon the floor that he spoke.

"I will help you," he said.

Mrs. Heaster closed her eyes and bowed her head. After a moment her shoulders began to tremble with silent tears.

***

"Surely, you don't believe her, Holmes," I said as we cantered along a by-road on a pair of horses the good lady had lent us. Holmes, astride a chestnut gelding, did not answer me as we made our way through sun-dappled lanes.

It was only after we had reached our Lewisburg inn and handed the horses off to a stable lad that Holmes stopped and looked first up at the darkening late afternoon blue of the American sky and then at me.

"Do you not?" he replied as if I had just asked my question this minute instead of an hour past.

I opened my mouth to reply, but Holmes would say no more.

14

The very next morning found us in the telegraph office where Holmes dictated a dozen telegrams and left me to pay the operator. We then went to municipal offices where Holmes demanded to speak to the county prosecutor, one Mr. John A. Preston. Upon presenting his credentials, Mr. Preston first raised bushy eyebrows in surprise and then shot to his feet.

"Dear me!" he said.

Holmes gave him a rueful smile. "I perceive that I am not entirely unknown even this far from London."

"Unknown! Good heavens, Mr. Holmes, but there is not a lawman in these United States who has not heard of the great Consulting Detective. Why, not eight months ago I attended a lecture in Norfolk on modern police procedure in which the lecturer thrice quoted from your monographs. I believe it's fair to say that the future of police and legal investigation will owe you a debt, sir."

Preston's words penetrated even Holmes's unusually unflappable cool and for a moment he was at a loss for words. "Why thank you, sir. If only Scotland Yard were as progressive in their thinking."

"Give them time, Mr. Holmes, give them time. A prophet is never accepted in his own country." Preston laughed at his own witticism and waved us to chairs. "What can I do for the great Mr. Sherlock Holmes?"

"I will get right to it, then," said Holmes, and he told Preston everything Mrs. Heaster had told us, even to the point of handing him her letter for examination. Preston chewed the fringe of his walrus mustache as he handed the letter back.

"Mrs. Heaster has already been to see me," he admitted.

"And have you done nothing?"

Preston cleared his throat. "To be honest, Mr. Holmes, superstition abounds in these parts. Though we are fairly modern here in Lewisburg, much of West Virginia is still wild, and a good many of my fellow citizens are deeply superstitious. Everyone has a tale of a ghost or goblin, and this would not be the first time I've had someone sitting in that very chair there telling me of knowledge shared with them from a friend or relative months or years in the grave. Wild-eyed kooks, Mr. Holmes. Superstitious country bumpkins."

"And is it your opinion, Mr. Preston, that Mrs. Heaster is another wild-eyed kook?" Holmes's tone was icy, for indeed the woman had impressed my friend with her calm clarity.

"Well," Preston said cautiously, "after all, her daughter's ghost . . . ?"

"You are not a believer?"

"I go to church," Preston said but would venture no further.

"You have, I hope, had at least the courtesy to read the transcript of the case, including the remarks of the county coroner?"

"No sir . . . I confess that I did not take the case seriously enough to care to investigate further."

"I do take it seriously," said Holmes with asperity.

They sat there on opposite sides of Preston's broad oak desk, and as I watched the prosecutor I realized it was possible for a seated man to give the impression of coming to full attention and even saluting without so much as moving his hands.

"If you will do me the courtesy of coming back tomorrow at ten o'clock," he said, "I will by then be fully familiar with this case."

Holmes stood. "Then we have no more to talk about until then, Mr. Preston. Good day." We left and outside Holmes gave me a wink. "I believe we have lit a fire there, Watson."

***

Preston was better than his word and had not only read the case but officially re-opened it. At Holmes's urging he sought approval from the judge to exhume the body of Zona Heaster-Shue. Holmes and I attended the autopsy, which was held in an empty schoolhouse, the children having been sent home for the day. It was the custom of West Virginia, perhaps of this part of America, for family members, witnesses, and the accused to all be present during the post mortem. I found this deeply unsettling, but Holmes was delighted by the opportunity to study Trout Shue in person for we had not yet met the gentleman in question.

He entered with a pair of burly constables behind him but Shue was so massive a man that he dwarfed the policemen. He had the huge shoulders and knotted muscles of a blacksmith. His hair and eyes were dark, and there was a cruel sensuality to his mouth. His jaw was thrust forward in resentment, and he made many a protestation of his innocence and expressed deep outrage at this unnecessary violation of his wife.

"I'll see you all in court for this!" he bellowed as we gathered around the body that lay exposed and defenseless on the makeshift table.

"I hope you shall," replied Holmes and the two men stared at each other for a long moment. I could feel electricity wash back and forth between them as if their spirits dueled with lightning bolts, parrying and thrusting on a metaphysical level while we watchers waited in the physical world.

Finally Shue curled his lip and turned away, the first to break eye contact. He flapped an arm in apparent disgust. "Do what you must. You will never prove anything."

I broke the ensuing silence by stepping to the coroner's side. "I am entirely at your disposal," I said. He nodded in evident relief, throwing worried looks at Shue.

We set about the dissection. Zona Heaster-Shue had been in the ground for weeks now, but her body was not nearly as decomposed as I had expected in this temperate climate. The flesh yielded to our blades as if the skin were yet infused with moisture. It was unnerving, and dare I say it—unnatural—but we plowed ahead.

We examined her all over but as we proceeded Holmes quietly said, "The throat, doctors. The throat."

We cut through the tissue to examine the tendons, cartilage and bone. The coroner gasped, but when he dictated his findings to the clerk his voice was steady.

***

"The discovery was made that the neck was broken and the windpipe mashed," said the coroner from the witness box in the courtroom. "On the throat were the marks of fingers indicating that she had been choked. The neck was dislocated between the first and second vertebrae. The ligaments were torn and ruptured. The windpipe had been crushed at a point in front of the neck."

From the spectators' gallery I watched as the findings struck home to each of the twelve jurors, and I saw several pairs of eyes flick toward Trout Shue, who sat behind the defense table, his face a study in cold contempt.

It was hot in the courtroom as the June sun beat down upon Lewisburg. Following the arrest of Trout Shue, Holmes and I had returned to England, but a summons from Mr. Preston had entreated us to return and so we had. Despite the autopsy findings it was by no means a certain victory for the prosecution. Shue at no time recanted his claim of innocence and the burden of proof in American law is entirely on the prosecution to establish without reasonable doubt that the accused was the murderer. The evidence as it currently stood was largely circumstantial. Overwhelming, it seemed to me, but in the eyes of the law things stood upon a knife-edge.

During a break in the trial Mrs. Heaster accosted Mr. Preston. "You must let me testify," she implored.

"To what end, madam? You were not a witness to the crime."

"But my daughter—"

Preston cut her off with some irritation, for in truth this was an argument they had revisited many times. "You claim your daughter came to you in a dream. A dream, madam."

"It was her ghost, sir. Her spirit cries out for justice."

Holmes gently interjected. "Mrs. Heaster, at very best this is hearsay and the laws of this country do not allow it as testimony. You cannot prove what you claim."

She wheeled on Holmes while pointing a finger at Preston. "Are you defending him? Are you saying that I should just be quiet and let my daughter's murderer glide through this trial like the oiled snake that he is?"

"Indeed not. In fact I have provided some evidence to Mr. Preston that he may find useful."

"What evidence," Mrs. Heaster and I said as one.

"Watson, do you remember that I sent a number of telegrams when we first arrived in Lewisburg?"

"Of course."

"I cabled various postmasters in this region in a search for forwarding addresses for anyone of the name Erasmus Stribbling Trout Shue, or any variation thereof, and I struck gold! It turns out our Trout Shue has quite a checkered past. He has already served time in jail on a previous occasion, being convicted of stealing a horse."

"That hardly bears on—"

Holmes brushed past my interruption. "Zona Heaster was not his first wife, Watson. Not even his second! Shue has been married twice before, and in both cases there were reports—"

"Unofficial reports," Preston interjected.

"Reports nevertheless," snapped Holmes, "that each of his previous wives suffered from the effects of his violent temper. His first wife divorced him after he had thrown all of her possessions into the street following an argument. She, of the three Mrs. Shue's, survived this man. Her successor was not so lucky."

"What do you mean?" demanded Mrs. Heaster.

"Lucy Ann Tritt, his second wife died under mysterious circumstances of a blow to the head, ostensibly from a fall—according to Shue, who was the only witness. The investigation in that case was as lax as it was here." Holmes gave Preston a harsh glare. "No charges were filed and Shue quickly moved away."

"And came here and found my Zona." She shivered and gripped Preston's sleeve. "You must secure a conviction, sir. This man is evil. Evil. Please, for the love of God, let me testify. Let me tell the jury about my daughter, about what she told me. Let me tell the truth!"

But Preston just shook his head. "Madam, I will try to introduce the evidence Mr. Holmes was clever enough to find, but it, too, is circumstantial. This man has not been convicted of harming any woman. I cannot even bring in his previous conviction for horse theft because it might prejudice the jury, and on those grounds the defense would declare a mistrial. I am bound by the law. And," he said tiredly, "I cannot in good conscience put you in the witness chair and have you give legal testimony that a ghost revealed to you in a dream that she was murdered. We would lose any credibility that we have, and already we are losing this jury. I thank my lucky stars that the defense has not learned of your claims, because then he would use it to tear our case apart."

"But the autopsy report—"

"Shows that she was murdered, but it does not establish the identity of the killer. I'm sorry, but please remember, the jury has to agree that there is no doubt, no doubt at all, that Shue is the killer. I do not know if we possess sufficient evidence to establish that." He began to pull her hand from his sleeve but held it for a moment and even gave it a gentle squeeze. "I will do everything that the law allows, madam. Everything."

She pulled her hand away. "The law! Where is justice in the law if it allows a girl to be murdered and her killer to walk free?" She looked at Preston, and at Holmes, and at me. "How many more women will he marry and then murder? How will the law protect them?"

I opened my mouth to mutter some meaningless words of comfort, but Mrs. Heaster whirled away and ran from us into a side room, her sobs echoing like accusations in the still air of the hallway.

Preston gave us a wretched look. "I can only do what the law allows," he pleaded.

Holmes smiled and clapped him on the shoulder. "We must trust that justice will find a way," he said. Then he consulted his watch. "Dear me, I'm late for luncheon."

And with that enigmatic statement he left us.

***

The trial ground on, and true to Preston's fears, the evidence became thinner and thinner. The defense attorney, a wily man named Grimby, seemed now to have taken possession of the jury's sympathies. Had I not looked into Shue's face during the autopsy and saw the cold calculation there, I might also have felt myself swayed into the region of reasonable doubt.

Again and again Mrs. Heaster begged Preston to let her testify, but each time the prosecutor denied her entreaties, and I could see his patience eroding as quickly as his optimism.

Then calamity struck.

When the judge asked Mr. Grimby if he had any additional witnesses, the defense attorney turned toward the prosecution table and with as wicked a smile as I'd ever seen on a man's face, said, "I call Mrs. Mary Jane Robinson Heaster."

The entire courtroom was struck into stunned silence. Preston closed his eyes, looking sick and defeated. He murmured, "Dear God, we are lost."

I wheeled toward Holmes, but my friend did not look at all discomfited. Instead he maintained what the Americans call a poker face—showing no trace of emotions, no hint of what thoughts were running through his brain during this disaster.

"Mrs. Heaster?" prompted the bailiff, offering his hand to her.

The good lady rose with great dignity though I could see her clenched fists trembling with dread. To have been denied the opportunity to speak against this evil man and now to become the tool of his advocate! It was unthinkably cruel.

"Holmes," I whispered. "Do something!"

Very calmly he said, "We have done all that can be done, Watson. We must trust to the spirit of justice."

Mrs. Heaster took the oath and sat in the witness chair, and immediately Grimby set about her, gainsaying niceties to close in for a quick kill. "Tell me, madam, do you believe that Mr. Shue had anything at all to do with your daughter's death?"

"I do, sir," she said quietly.

"Did you witness her death?"

"No, sir."

"Did you speak to anyone who witnessed her death?"

"No, sir."

"So you have no personal knowledge of the manner of your daughter's death?"

She paused.

"Come now, Mrs. Heaster, it's a simple question. Do you have any personal knowledge of how your daughter died?"

"Yes," she said at length. "I do."

Grimby's eyes were alight and he fought to keep a smile off of his face. "And how do you come by this knowledge?"

"I was told."

"Told? By whom, madam?" His voice dripped with condescension.

"By my daughter, sir."

Grimby smiled openly now. "Your . . . dead daughter?"

"Yes sir."

"Are we to understand that your dead daughter somehow imparted this information to you?"

"Yes, my daughter told me how she died."

The jury gasped. Preston could have objected here, but he had lost his nerve, clearly believing the case to be already lost.

"Pray, how did she tell you?"

Mrs. Heaster raised her eyes to meet Grimby's. "Her ghost came to me in a dream, sir."

"Her ghost?" Grimby cried. "In a dream?"

There was a ripple of laughter from the gallery and even a few smiles from the jury. Preston's fists were clutched so tight his knuckles were bloodless; while to my other side Holmes sat composed, his eyes fixed on the side of Mrs. Heaster's face.

Grimby opened his mouth to say something to the judge, but Mrs. Heaster cut him off. "You may laugh, sir. You may all laugh, for perhaps to you it is funny. A young woman dies a horrible death, the life choked out of her, the very bones of her neck crushed in the fingers of a strong man. That may be funny to some." The laughter in the room died away. "My daughter was a good girl who had endured a hard life. Yes, she made mistakes. Mr. Grimby has been kind enough to detail each and every one of them. Yes, she had a child out of wedlock, and as we all know, such things are unthinkable, such things never happen."

Her bitterness was like a pall of smoke.

"Mr. Grimby did his job very well and dismantled the good name of my daughter while at the same time destroying each separate bit of evidence. Perhaps most of you have already made up your minds and are planning to set Trout Shue free." She paused and flicked a glance at Holmes, and did I catch just the slightest incline of his head? "The law prevents me from telling what I know of Mr. Shue's life and dealings before he came to Greenbrier. So I will not talk of him. Mr. Grimby has asked me to tell you how I came by my personal knowledge of the death of my daughter, and so I will tell you. I will tell you of how my dear Zona came to me over the course of four dark nights. As a spirit of the dead she came into my room and stood at my bedside, the way a frightened child will do, coming to the one person who loves her unconditionally and forever. For four nights she came to me, and she brought with her the chill of the grave. The very air around me seemed to freeze, and the ghost of each of my frightened breaths haunted the air for, yes, I was afraid. Terribly afraid. I am not a fanciful woman. I am not one to knock wood or throw salt in the devil's eye over my left shoulder. I am a mountain woman of Greenbrier County. A farmwoman with a practical mind. And yet there I lay in my bed with the air turned to winter around me and the shade of my murdered daughter standing beside me."

The room was silent as the grave as she spoke.

"Each night she would awaken me and then she would tell me, over and over again, how she died. And how she lived. How she endured life in those last months as the wife of Edward Trout Shue. She told me of the endless fights over the smallest matters. Of his insane jealousy if she so much as curtsied in reply to a gentleman tipping his hat. Of the beatings that he laid upon her, and how he cleverly chose where and how to hit so that he left no marks that would show above collar or below sleeve. My daughter lived in hell. Constant fear, constant dread of offending this offensive man. And then she told me what happened on that terrible day. Trout Shue had come home from the blacksmiths, expecting his dinner, and when he found that she had not yet prepared it—even though he was two hours earlier than his usual time—he flew into a rage and grabbed her by the throat. His eyes flared like a monster's and she said his hands were as hard and unyielding as the iron with which he plied his trade. He did not just throttle my daughter—he shattered her neck. When I dared speak, when I dared to ask her to show me what his hands had done, Zona turned her head to one side. At first I thought she was turning away in shame and horror for what had happened . . . but as she turned her head went far to the left—and too far. Much too far and with a grinding of broken bones Zona turned her head all the way around. If anything could be more horrible, more unnatural, more dreadful to a human heart, let alone the broken heart of a grieving mother, then I do not want to know what it could be."

She paused. Her eyes glistened with tears but her voice never disintegrated into hysterics or even rose above a normal speaking tone. The effect was to make her words a hundredfold more potent. Any ranting would have painted her as overly distraught if not mad, but now everyone in the courtroom hung on her words. Even Grimby seemed caught up in it. I hazarded a glance at Shue, who looked—for the very first time—uncertain.

"I screamed," said Mrs. Heaster. "Of course I did. Who would not? Nothing in my life had prepared me for so ghastly a sight as this. After that first night I convinced myself that it had all been a hysterical dream, that such things as phantoms did not exist and that my Zona was not haunting me, but on that second night she returned. Once more she begged me to hear the truth about what happened, and once more she told me of the awful attack. I only thank God that I was not again subjected to the demonstration of the extent of damage to her poor, dear neck." She paused and gave the jury a small, sad smile. "I pleaded with Mr. Preston to let me tell my tale during this trial and he refused. I fear he was afraid that my words would make you laugh at me. I believe Mr. Grimby placed me on the stand for those very reasons. And yet I hear no laughter, I see no smiles. Perhaps it is that you, like I, do not find the terrible and painful death of an innocent girl to be a source of merriment. In any case, I have had my say, and for that I thank Mr. Grimby and this court. At least now, no matter what you each decide, my daughter has been heard. For me that will have to be enough."

She looked at Grimby, who in turn looked at the jury. He saw what I saw: twelve faces whose eyes were moist but whose mouths had become tight with bitter lines. Outthrust jaws bespoke their fury.

Then the silence was shattered as Shue himself leapt to his feet and cried, "Tell whatever fairytales you want, woman, but you will never be able to prove I did it!"

The guards shoved him down in his seat and Holmes leaned his head toward Preston and me. "Do you not find it an interesting choice of phrase that he said that we will never 'prove' he did it? Does that sound like the plea of an innocent man or the challenge of a guilty one?" And though he said this quietly, he pitched it just loud enough to be heard by everyone in that small and crowded room.

**

That was very nearly the end of the Greenbrier affair, and Holmes and I left West Virginia and America very shortly thereafter. Erasmus Stribbling Trout Shue was found guilty by the jury, which returned its verdict with astonishing swiftness. The judge, with fury and revulsion in his eyes, sentenced Shue to life imprisonment in the State Penitentiary in Moundsville, where Shue died some three years later of a disease that was never adequately diagnosed. Mr. Preston sent Holmes a newspaper account from Lewisburg after Shue's death in which the reporter recounted a rumor that Shue complained that a ghost visited him nightly, and as a result, he was unable to sleep. His health deteriorated, and when he died, he was buried in an unmarked grave. No one that I knew of attended the burial or mourned his passing.

But before Holmes and I had even set out from Lewisburg, as we shared a late dinner in our rooms at the hotel, I said, "There is one thing that confounds me, Holmes."

"Only one thing? And pray what is that?"

"How did Mr. Grimby know to ask Mrs. Heaster about her story? It was not commonly known as far as I could tell, especially not here in Lewisburg. Certainly neither she nor Mr. Preston shared that information."

Holmes ate a bit of roast duck and washed it down with wine before he answered. "Does it matter how he found out? Perhaps he learned of it from a ghost in his dreams."

I opened my mouth to reply that it surely did matter when an odd thought struck me dumb. I gaped accusingly at Holmes and set my knife and fork down with a crash.

"If it was someone on this physical plane who tipped him off, then it was criminal to do so! The risk was abominable. What if she had raved?"

"We have not once seen Mrs. Heaster rave," he observed calmly. "Rather the reverse."

"What if the jury did not believe her? What if Grimby had managed her better on the stand? What if—?"

Holmes cut me off. "What if once in a while, Watson, justice was more important in a court of law than the law itself?" He sipped his wine.

Once more I opened my mouth to protest, but then a chill wind seemed to blow through the room, making the curtains dance and causing the candle flames to flicker, and in that moment I could feel the heat of my outrage and anger leak out of me. Holmes cut another slice of duck and ate it, his glittering dark eyes dancing with a strange humor. I followed the line of his gaze and saw that he was looking at the curtains, watching as they settled back into place, and then the chill of the room seemed to touch my chest like the cold hand of a dead child over my heart. Though the day had been a hot one, the night had been cool, and the maid had shut the window against the breeze. The curtains hung now, as still as if they had never moved, for indeed they could not have.

When I turned back to Holmes, he was looking at me now, half a smile on his mouth.

Was it a breeze that had found its way through the window frame, or perhaps through an unseen crack in the wall? Or had some voiceless mouth whispered thank you to Holmes in the language of the grave? I will not say what I think nor commit it to paper.

We said nothing for the rest of that evening, and in the morning we took ship for England, leaving Greenbrier and the ghosts of West Virginia far behind.

The Grim Beast of Iaeger

Bob Freeman

Bob Freeman is an author, illustrator, and paranormal adventurer who lives in rural Indiana with his wife Kim, son Connor, and sister-in-law Cassie. He is the President of Indiana Horror Writers, a member of the Horror Writers Association, and the Aleister Crowley Society. Bob can be found online at www.cairnwood.net.

Gather 'round the fire, children, for I have a tale to tell about a night not unlike the one that wraps around us now, with a moon hidden behind the thick veil of a sinister storm and the promise of an unrelenting torrent. Can you hear it on the wind? Does your spine tingle with dread and an anticipation of grim reminders of days long past, when the wild was just beyond the light, lurking in the shadows? Draw close to one another, for there's safety in numbers, and that's a lesson that could have served a young girl on a cold, godless night had she been of a mind to trust in it. Her name was Dawn Sevier and this is as much her story as it is of the strange happenings that haunted this tortured landscape but a short time past, and haunt it still if you believe in such things that do more than just go bump in the night. Sometimes those things can bite.

Dawn Sevier was pretty, popular, and quite possibly pregnant. Witnesses placed her in the Iaeger Pharmacy purchasing a home pregnancy test soon after the Cubs' narrow win over the Big Creek Owls, thanks to a miraculous pass that slipped through the hands of an Owl defender and found quarterback Danny Chaplin's favorite receiver in the end zone for a last-second touchdown. It can be surmised that Dawn feared that Danny had made another miraculous touchdown pass some weeks earlier in the backseat of his Cutlass Supreme. The two young lovers had a heated exchange on the walk bridge that traversed the Tug. When they finally parted company, Danny joined his friends in front of Iaeger Supply, drinking warm Pabst Blue Ribbon, while Dawn stormed off tearfully into the fractured night.

As morning light spread across the small hamlet, there was no Dawn to be found and the inhabitants of Iaeger were quick to gather together, not only to support a distraught family during their time of despair, but also to join in the search for one of their own. As their attempts at finding the teen turned fruitless, a murmur spread through the community, passed by superstitious lips that had seen more than their fair share of strange happenings in this neck of the woods, and their fears were amplified when Delbert Gentry came forward. Delbert had been driving along Sandy Huff Road late that Friday night, off to do a spot of 'coon hunting with his dogs in tow, when he'd spotted a chestnut-haired cheerleader walking along the loose berm. He stopped and offered the girl a ride, but she'd refused.

The road through Sandy Huff Hollow weaved through the wilderness like a feral snake and was steeped in local lore as place where the dead were restless. When night fell on the Hollow it was transformed they said into a haunted place where none but the bravest of souls dared pass. Dawn Sevier knew well to steer clear of such a dreadful place, but in her distress it seemed she'd sought solace among the tormented spirits that called the Hollow their home. Why, I can almost hear their anguished wails even now, drifting across the wilds. Can you hear them? Listen close, children. No, it's more than the lament of the ghosts that haunt those woods, it's something even more sinister, more terrifying. It's the very embodiment of the primal night itself.

Surely you've heard the tales of the grim beast that makes the Hollow its home? Some say the ghosts that haunt Sandy Huff are the victims of the dread beast, who wail in eternal agony over their horrific demise from the claws and fangs of the unspeakable creature. I hear tell that many a hunter has spied the beast, often rearing up on its hind legs and tearing through the woods with its dog-like maw snapping viciously. Yes, children, more than one man has been chased from the Hollow by this terrible beast. What then of a poor defenseless girl, in a state of remorse over a life that had taken an unexpected turn? What hope would she have against such an unnatural creature?

It was on the fourth night of Dawn's disappearance that Danny Chaplain, broken hearted and riddled with guilt, stalked off into the Hollow with revenge on his mind despite the warnings and pleas of his friends and family. Armed with a 12-gauge pump, Danny entered the haunted woodland, hoping against hope that he might find his girlfriend alive, but with the nagging feeling in his gut that something far more sinister had happened to his lost love.

Hours later, nestled in the relative safety of their small town, the inhabitants of Iaeger heard shotgun blasts echoing down from Sandy Huff Hollow, and when first light broke, the searchers returned to the woods, but Dawn was still nowhere to be found. Instead they found the mangled body of Danny Chaplain, his entrails spilled out across the forest floor, his face frozen in abject terror. Clutched in his hand . . . a ragged and torn remnant from a blue and gold cheerleader uniform, dripping with blood.

Let this be a lesson to you, children, should you ever think that you're brave enough to enter into Sandy Huff Hollow alone. There is a grim beast that calls the Hollow its home, and should you draw its attention, there can be but one outcome. So cling to one another and say your prayers, and if you ever find yourself with a curiosity about what may lurk in the shadows of the wilds, remember Dawn Sevier and Danny Chaplain. In the dark and quiet places there are things that are better left alone. That is, if you've a mind to live to see another sunrise. Now, off to bed with the lot of you, but keep an eye open and an ear to the ground . . . and remember . . . there's safety in numbers. Sandy Huff Hollow is no place to walk alone.

The Cold Gallery

Lucy A. Snyder

Lucy A. Snyder is the author of the collections *Sparks and Shadows* and *Installing Linux on a Dead Badger*; Del Rey will release her urban fantasy novel *Spellbent* in 2009. Her work has appeared in a wide variety of publications, including *Strange Horizons*, *Chiaroscuro*, and *Masques V*. Visit www.lucysnyder.com for more information.

Emma and her mother joined the line of kids and parents in Riggleman Hall's foyer. They'd be waiting a while. The Freshman Orientation coordinators had scheduled far too few advisors for far too many students.

Suddenly, a chill crept across Emma's back, and she felt a pair of icy hands close around her neck.

"Hey!" She whirled around.

"What's the matter?" Her mom looked puzzled.

"Someone. . ." Emma trailed off. Not only was nobody standing behind her, nobody was within twenty feet of her. "Nothing. Just my nerves, I guess."

***

"Well, this is nice." Emma's mother led the way into the dorm room and plunked down the duffel bag. "Very nice, don't you think?"

"Um. . ." Emma set down her suitcases. The relentlessly beige room was smaller than it had looked on the university website. At least she had the place to herself. "Yeah, it seems nice, Mom."

"The dorms we had weren't nearly this spacious."

Looking wistful, her mom opened her purse and pulled out the letter from her father, Professor Burke.

Her father. It felt weird to even think the words. It was easier to think of him as the Professor. Growing up, the other kids at her school had fathers or stepfathers or erstwhile "uncles," but never Emma. She couldn't even remember her mom ever going on a date. Of course, with her mom's grindingly long shifts at the hospital, it would have been hard for her to have much of a social life.

And that, at least according to her Aunt Mary, was entirely her father's fault.

Emma's mom rarely spoke of him, but her aunt wasn't one to mince words or keep silent. According to Mary, her father was Edgar Burke, a chemistry instructor who dumped her mother when she got pregnant. Emma's mom had to drop out of college and go to work as a nurses' aide while he went on to become a full professor with a fat salary. Mary wanted her sister to sue for child support, but Emma's mother never followed up with the lawyers Mary contacted on her behalf.

It seemed the good Professor was determined to have nothing to do with his daughter. But on her 16th birthday, a FedEx guy delivered a fancy basket of Godiva chocolates to their little clapboard rental in Huntington. That night, Burke telephoned the house, and Emma had her first, awkward conversation with the man who until that day had only given her half her genes.

The support checks came Johnny-on-the-spot after that. And on her next birthday, right when Emma and her mother were starting to fret over college costs, he offered to pay for Emma to attend UC.

"Your father wants to meet with you in his office at noon tomorrow," her mom said, reading over the letter. "He's in Clay Tower."

Emma suddenly felt nervous. She'd talked to the Professor at most six times on the phone, and he'd been away at a conference when she and her mom visited the campus before. "Are . . . are you going to come with me?"

Her mother's smile faded for the briefest second. "No, honey, I . . . I have to be back at the hospital tomorrow. Look, it'll be fine! Just be your regular sweet self. We can thank the Lord that he's changed his ways and found the love of Jesus in his heart to finally do right by you."

***

There were no crosses in Professor Burke's office. Nor were there any Christian books that Emma could see in the floor-to-ceiling oak shelves that lined every inch of wall space beyond the doorway and wide window. The *Encyclopedia Paranormal* volumes and books on Voudun and Medieval witchcraft scattered amongst the organic chemistry and mathematics texts counted as a sort of religious reading, Emma supposed, but surely not the kind that involved Jesus or love.

The professor himself was sitting behind a wide desk, engrossed in a science journal. He was a lean, well-kept man in his late 40s or early 50s, and he was dressed much more stylishly than she'd expected. His handsome face was an odd mix of the strange and familiar: his nose and full lips were masculine versions of hers, and she'd seen his gray eyes in every mirror.

Emma wiped her sweaty palms on her khaki skirt and cleared her throat. Burke finally looked up and noticed her standing in the doorway. His face broke into a smile as broad and bright as the noon sun over Antarctica.

"You must be Emma," he said, standing and gesturing toward one of the high-backed chairs in front of his desk. "Please, come in and have a seat. So, you're settled in the dormitory okay? Got all the classes you wanted to take?"

"Yes sir," she said as she sat down.

"Good, good." He opened one of his desk drawers and pulled out a sheet of paper. "I took the liberty of getting you a job here on campus at the Erma Byrd Art Gallery. It's just ten hours a week, and they'll work around your schedule. I'm sure you could use a bit of pocket money, and it will look good on your resumé."

He passed the paper to her; it was a job acceptance letter signed by the museum curator. All official and addressed to her, just as if she'd applied on her own. She was going to be an evening attendant, whatever that meant.

***

The art gallery was in Riggleman Hall; the tall, dark windows striping the building seemed much more ominous than they had the day before. Inside, it felt like the building's AC was cranked up too high, although students jostling past her on the first floor were complaining about the heat. Emma took the stairs to try to warm up, but she felt even colder by the time she got to the gallery.

The curator, Mrs. Plymale, was a bright, cheery woman in her mid-30s.

"What you'll mostly be doing is keeping an eye on things and answering questions," she told Emma. "I'll give you a packet of information about all our artists and the paintings on display. It's usually pretty quiet here, but we'll give you a walkie-talkie in case you need to call maintenance or security. Also, we have special events like weddings on some weekends, and we'll need help setting up and tearing down. Nothing very hard or intense."

Emma had been rubbing her arms to try to warm them a little. Mrs. Plymale seemed to notice her goosebumps.

"Is it cold to you in here?" the curator asked. She was wearing a light, sleeveless dress. There was a faint sheen of perspiration at the base of her neck.

Emma nodded. "A little."

Mrs. Plymale smiled sympathetically. "It's like that for some people who are . . . sensitive, I guess is the best word. My advice is, don't stay too long after your shift is over. It might be worse after dark."

"Worse? How?"

Mrs. Plymale held up both hands. "Mind you, I haven't felt anything weird myself, so I don't put that much stock in stories of this place being haunted. But people have sworn they've heard voices, felt strange touches and cold spots. Things like that. Mostly after sunset."

"The building is haunted? By what?"

The curator laughed uncomfortably. "There's a story that a girl died. Killed herself when she found out she was pregnant. Some people say she jumped off the roof, others say she poisoned herself. Lots of rumors, not much evidence. They wouldn't be able to keep a student's death out of the papers nowadays, but decades ago . . . well, who knows what might have happened here?"

***

Emma's first shift in the gallery was deadly slow. Two visitors came her first hour, and nobody after that. She'd brought a cotton jacket with her, but the chill got to her after a while and she spent the last hour pacing up and down the glossy checkerboard floor, reading Mrs. Plymale's handout on

West Virginia Women Artists.

Afterward, she decided to take the stairs back to the ground floor. The hallway door had just shut behind her on the landing when she thought she heard a whisper.

Blood for blood.

A wave of cold vertigo hit her, and suddenly she pitched forward, arms windmilling, barely able to catch herself on the safety rail. Trembling, she got to her feet, her wrenched shoulder aching sharply. She was alone; surely the disembodied voice had just been her imagination.

But her fall could have been far from imaginary. If she'd missed that railing, she'd have gone headfirst down the stairs, probably breaking her neck in the process.

No more stairs for her, not if she could help it.

***

Her next shift involved a few more visitors, but the last hour was just as quiet as before. She began to circle the gallery, looking at the paintings.

On her third circuit, she saw something on the wall she was sure hadn't been there before. It was a charcoal drawing in a battered round frame. It depicted a man and a woman watching a sunset from atop a square building with long, dark windows. Riggleman Hall, Emma realized. The drawing was amateur compared to the rest of the works in the gallery, but something about it kept her riveted.

The shivery vertigo took her again, and suddenly she was standing on the roof, gazing into the grey eyes of a handsome, wispy-bearded, shaggy-haired boy of 18 or 19. He wore a butterfly collared green shirt and bell-bottoms.

He was shaking his head at her. "We can't have a kid, Linda. I'm not even close to being done with school; I can't be tied down right now. I'll drive you to Columbus. We can get it taken care of up there and your folks will never—"

"No," she heard herself say. "I'm havin' our baby, and you're gonna be a man for a change and do the right thing."

A cold, hard anger gleamed in his eyes. No love there. "You don't get to push me around, girl."

"Fine." She turned and began to walk away across the gravel rooftop. "We'll see what your Pa has to say."

Suddenly he grabbed her arm and jerked her sideways, nearly off her feet. Eddie was stronger than she'd expected, too strong to resist. In a heartbeat he'd thrown her off the building and she was tumbling through the air, the merciless concrete steps rising to meet her—

Emma was back in her own body, crumpled on the floor beneath the enchanted painting.

Blood for blood, the murdered girl's voice whispered inside her head. If I can't have him, I'll take you.

Emma felt the ghost's tormented emotions burning like rattlesnake venom in her veins. The pain of betrayal. Rage over her destroyed future, lost motherhood, forgotten name. And blind hatred for Emma, her murdering lover's child, the adored daughter of the relationship that should have been hers—

"No," Emma gasped, her heart twitching jaggedly in her chest. "That's not how it's been. Please, listen."

She opened her memories to the ghost, praying Linda wasn't so bent on vengeance she wouldn't care about the truth. . .

***

"Come in; it's not locked."

Professor Burke looked supremely surprised to see his daughter push open his office door.

"Emma? I didn't expect—"

"That I'd still be alive? Us girls, we're full of surprises, huh? Can't count on us to save you from thirty-year-old blood curses or anything."

"What?"

"I really appreciate being used as ghost bait, Dad. And Linda, she sure appreciates being murdered."

The color had drained from his face. "I don't know what you're talking about."

"Really? Maybe this will jog your memory."

She pulled Linda's drawing from its hiding place under her jacket and turned the image toward her father.

At least fifty people crowded outside the police tape surrounding Professor Burke's broken body at the base of Clay Tower: tired-looking EMTs, grim-faced cops, whispering faculty, and students surreptitiously filming the carnage with their cell phones.

"So you're saying he threw the chair through his window, and jumped out after it?" the police detective asked Emma.

"Yes, sir."

"And he didn't say why?"

"I . . . didn't know my father very well," she replied. "Maybe something was bothering him that he never talked about."

"Maybe." The detective flipped his notebook closed. "In any case, I'm sorry for your loss, Miss."

In a strange way, Emma realized, so was she.

The Anniversary

Nate Kenyon

Nate Kenyon is the author of the Stoker-nominated *Bloodstone* and *The Reach* (Leisure Books). He has published short fiction in *Terminal Frights*, the *Monstros* anthology, and *Shroud Magazine*, among others. Visit his website at www.natekenyon.com.

"Gets pretty quiet after ten," Officer Shields said. They were walking past three deserted cells on their way back to the front, and Jeffrey glanced in at the empty bunk beds, stained toilets and cracked cement. "No prisoners for you to worry about tonight," Shields said. "And you won't get more than one or two calls, if that. Most everyone in town's asleep already."

It was just about what Jeffrey expected. Beautiful old town, but quiet as the dead. Before moving here he'd worked as a beat cop in Charleston and had to be on his guard constantly or risk getting shot, usually by a bunch of gang bangers not too far removed from junior high. Those bangers with the dead-eyed stares had scared the hell out of him. His new assignment on the nightshift in this backwater town of Harper's Ferry would be a welcome change of pace, which was one reason he'd asked to be transferred in the first place.

One of the reasons.

"Two cars out on patrol," Shields said. "They'll call in if they need you. Give 'em a holler every couple hours to keep 'em awake."

In the outer office the two rows of cluttered desks sat empty. A middle-aged woman with hair like steel wool and a body swallowed by her uniform thumped the door open with her rear end, while fishing in her pocketbook for her car keys. A man with mottled cheeks and a deep cleft in his chin (Officer Thomas, if Jeffrey remembered correctly) approached them a moment later, shrugging into his black raincoat. "I'm off, Harry. You got the new man all settled, I guess."

Officer Shields put his hand on Jeffrey's upper arm. "Doin' just fine."

Thomas stopped in front of them and adjusted his belt over his belly.

"He'll be alone?"

"Of course he will."

"It's the anniversary tonight, is all."

"I know it."

"You gonna tell him?"

"First timers never hear it anyway."

"Sometimes they do. You should warn him is all I'm saying."

"Warn me about what?"

"Oh," Shields said vaguely, "an old superstition is what Mr. Thomas here is getting at. Nothing for you to worry about."

"Worry." Thomas grunted. "First time I heard the ghost train I nearly soiled my shorts."

"What Claude is trying to say is that every once in a while you get a noise that sounds like a train going down the old tracks west of town," Shields explained. He waved a hand in the air like this was the most natural thing in the world.

"But trains haven't come through that area in years, have they? The freights all take the bridge."

"I said it sounds like a train. A trick of the wind."

"You ought to know the story," Thomas said. "You can decide for yourself whether it's a trick of the wind or not."

The three of them stood in a small circle. They were alone in the station. Beyond the glass doors the street sat quiet and empty and dark.

Officer Shields frowned, but Thomas didn't pay him any attention. "Long time ago," Thomas said, "the trains used to come through there regular, just came whipping through like a bat out of hell. Anyway, one night a little girl was out walking with her daddy near the tracks, real late. Girl was maybe six or seven years old. It was foggy, kind of like tonight."

Jeffrey glanced out the glass doors. Tendrils of white drifted around the front steps and the two or three cars still parked near the entrance. "So what happened?"

"Her daddy must have gotten turned around. One of them big old freights came rumbling down and with the fog and all, and the headlight coming at him like some kind of devil—"

"He was killed," Shields said. "A terrible tragedy, and one of the reasons they moved the track."

"Spread him across about a quarter mile," Thomas continued unperturbed, as if Shields hadn't spoken. "A while later the little girl wanders into the station, asking the nightshift man for help. Her daddy had gotten chased by a monster with a big glowing eye, she said. Well, the officer on duty knew what had happened right off. They found his body around daybreak, or what was left of it."

"Why were they out so late?"

"Nobody knows. Some think the man might have been trying to commit suicide and was taking his daughter with him, only she got away at the last minute."

"Claude, I think that's enough—"

"Tonight's the anniversary of the accident, see," Thomas said, a little louder now. "Every year around midnight, on the night it happened, you can hear the train going through. You can hear it whistle just like that poor scumbag must have, just before it hit him."

"You're kidding me," Jeffrey said.

"I wouldn't kid about a thing like that. And Shields here, he'd tell you if it was BS, but he won't, 'cause it ain't.'" Thomas looked at the other man, who shrugged. "See what I'm saying?"

It was a heck of a story, Jeffrey thought. "And you say you've heard it before? The train?"

"Sure. And tonight's special," Thomas said. "One hundred fifty years exactly. They say it's extra strong on nights like this."

"A trick of the wind," Shields said. The top of his head had gone a curious shade of pink.

They stood in silence, then Thomas laughed and clapped Jeffrey on the back. "Didn't mean to scare you," he said. "But I wouldn't want you to hear that train and go wandering around out in the fog looking for it. A man could get lost doing a thing like that."

***

After the two men left, Jeffrey sat at his new desk for a while, trying to read the newspaper. His eyes kept straying from the page up to the clock on the wall. Was being stranded out here in the middle of nowhere really better than the city?

You might be bored to tears, but at least it's safe. About a month ago he'd stumbled upon a drug deal under an overpass. One of the participants pulled a .38 and chipped the concrete about three feet from Jeffrey's head before his partner took him down with a flying tackle. The shooter was a thirteen-year-old.

That was the sort of thing that would make you reassess your life.

He called the cars on patrol, and felt pretty sure he'd woken up the second driver from a sound sleep. At ten-thirty he got up and wandered around, having another look at the jail cells. Someone had taped a page from a men's magazine to the wall under the top bunk of the last cell. The naked woman in the picture was smiling invitingly out at the camera.

Jeffrey returned to the front room, put his feet up on the desk, and tried not to think of his girlfriend. She'd been getting too serious with him lately, talking about settling down and starting a family. He didn't want to hurt her, but he was only twenty-six. He'd always thought that when the right girl came along, he'd know it as soon as he laid eyes on her face.

It hadn't happened yet.

Maybe this nightshift wasn't such a good idea after all. Maybe he needed a little excitement to keep him from nodding off, and to occupy his mind with anything other than his relationship with Sheila.

Outside the station the fog had thickened, so that it was now impossible to make out more than the dim, hulking shape of the lone remaining vehicle parked at the curb. He watched the street for two full minutes but nothing passed by and the scene did not change. Jeffrey felt like the only person on earth left alive.

Quite a story Thomas had told. Ghost train, indeed. Though he wondered about the little girl and her dead father. Why had they been wandering the train tracks at such a late hour? People simply did not go for a leisurely walk at midnight on a foggy, cold night. The girl's father had been up to something, all right. Perhaps suicide was the answer.

When his cell phone rang he nearly lost his balance and toppled over in his chair.

"How's the new job?"

Oh, Christ. Sheila. "Fascinating," he said. He glanced at no smoking sign on the wall, then held the phone to his ear with his shoulder as he lit a cigarette. "I should have brought Monopoly. But then I'd be playing with myself."

"I could help you out there." A teasing lilt in her voice. "I've done it before."

"A little far away for that, aren't you?"

"I guess so. I miss you."

"I know you do."

He waited through an uncomfortable silence.

"So," she said, "I expected you to call me tonight."

"I've been working."

"Don't tell me you forgot. It's our anniversary. Do you remember the day we met? That was one year to this day. A year is a long time to be seeing someone. We've been through a lot, haven't we? I feel like we know each other so well. It's like we were meant to be together."

A drop of sweat trickled inside the collar of Jeffrey's uniform. He wiped at his neck and ground the cigarette out on his heel.

"You did forget, didn't you? I can't believe it."

"I'm sorry, it's just that I've been trying to settle in here and—"

"Is there room in your new apartment for a weekend visitor? I was thinking I'd take a train there, check things out. I'm a city girl at heart, but who knows, maybe if I get a whiff of that country air I'll fall in love."

"I've got an extra shift."

"Why are you avoiding this, Jeff?" Her voice raised an octave in pitch. "Is there someone else? Is that it?"

"Of course not, it's just, I don't know. . ."

"Then what?"

"Sheila, I'm trying to work here. I gotta go."

"Fine," she said. "Call me later, okay? I just . . . we have to talk. Please?"

***

At one point Jeffrey put his head down to rest his eyes, and he must have nodded off because the next thing he heard was the sound of a girl crying. He couldn't place the location at first; it seemed to come from all around him. A symptom of the fog, he thought. Having it swirling around just beyond the door was disorienting, as if the rest of the world was slowly being erased.

The crying did not stop. He thought about the ghost train. Surely the two men were playing a trick on him. He got up and looked into the corners of the room for loudspeakers or a CD player, but didn't see any.

When he turned around again the little girl was standing just outside the glass doors. She wore a white dress with a small dark bow at the breast. Her hair was the color of snow during the full moon. She had her hands against the glass and was staring in at him, tears coursing down her pretty face.

Jeffrey almost cried out but stopped himself. Thomas was really having a good laugh, he thought. They must have gone to great lengths to pull off such a prank. Some sort of initiation ritual for the new man. Nevertheless he had to swallow hard over the lump in his throat as he walked quickly toward the door.

It was cruel what they were doing to her, anyone could see that. A little girl out this late by herself, crying the way she was, with nobody to see to her.

When he opened the door the fog crept in and swirled around his ankles. The little girl's eyes were dark and huge and shining. "Help me," she said. "My daddy's lost and I can't find him."

A terrible thing, Jeffrey thought again, what they're doing. He crouched and touched the girl's cheek. It was cold and wet. Real flesh, real tears, of course. No such thing as ghosts.

Somewhere far away, he heard a sound like a distant moan.

"You don't have to do this," he said firmly. "Whatever they told you it wasn't true."

Tears rolled thickly down the girl's cheeks. "We were out walking and then a big monster came and my daddy ran." She grabbed his hand and started tugging at him. "Please help me find him."

Jeffrey allowed himself to be led away from the circle of light by the door. "Wherever you are out there," he said loudly, as they slipped down the steps, the girl pulling him towards the street, "I want you to know this isn't funny."

Nobody answered, but of course he didn't expect that. They passed his car and were quickly submerged in a world of white fog. A moment later they left the pavement and began walking through high grass. He could barely see the little girl and her white dress as she led him on, but she didn't falter.

He wondered what time it was. The fog was too thick to see anything. He smelled wet soil and decaying leaves. Was the land tilting under his feet?

This was too much. Maybe it wasn't an initiation thing at all, but a test. If he wasn't at his post when Shields returned, he'd be fired.

He felt the dainty bones of the little girl's hand in his own. He felt an overwhelming need to protect her; she was so small and so helpless, and he was all she had.

He stumbled and the girl pulled him up again. She was moving faster now, her grip on him harder than before. His hand had gone numb with cold, and now his blood began to thud in his temples. He could feel each heartbeat shake his chest.

This time when the sound came it was much louder. Along with it came a slight tremor in the ground under his feet. "Close now," the little girl said eagerly. She was looking back at him over her shoulder. "Come on."

"No," Jeffrey said. "This was a mistake."

The girl stopped. Then she looked up and smiled. "It's just a little farther. Please."

"I'm sorry, honey. We'll go back and use the telephone. We'll call your house. It's going to be okay."

She shook her head. "We can't go back now."

Jeffrey's throat had gone tight. "Thomas!" he shouted. The fog swallowed his voice. "Shields! Get out here!"

His cell phone chirped and he jumped. He'd forgotten it was in his pocket. Thank God.

"Jeffrey? Hello? Are you there? It's Sheila again. Listen, I have something important to tell you and it can't wait."

Jeffrey felt lightheaded. The prickling, itching feeling at the back of his neck and under his arms was unbearable. He thought he might be sick.

"Oh, God," she said in a rush, as the phone buzzed in and out, "I'm sorry. I'm so sorry. I didn't want to tell you like this. It was supposed to be special. It's just that you're acting so distant."

"No," he managed numbly. "It's my fault."

"I don't know what to do! We need to talk face to face. Jeff? Jeff?" The phone hissed as her voice faded and the connection died.

"Will you help me find my daddy?"

The girl. Jeffrey had almost forgotten she was there. He realized he was standing on something uneven. Old railroad trestles crossed under his shoes. A humming vibrated up through his legs and weakened his limbs.

There's a train coming, he thought. I don't know how and I don't know why but there is.

He looked down at the girl. The ground was shaking now. Light bathed them both, turning the high grass white and reflecting off the fog so that it came from all directions at once. Jeffrey tried to pull away as a whistle split the silence, but the girl's hand yanked him back onto the tracks.

When he looked at her again her face had changed into something dark and smooth and vicious.

He caught a glimpse of glittering eyes and sharp bony teeth. She swelled, rose up and loomed over him like a great flapping shadow. Her arms enfolded him and drew him close.

The cell phone clattered onto the tracks. Jeffrey screamed. The approaching train bore down like thunder and the whistle sounded again. He realized what had really happened that night 150 years ago.

The little girl's daddy hadn't been trying to commit suicide when the train had run him down.

He had been trying to get away.

Cain Twists

Steven L. Shrewsbury

Steven L. Shrewsbury lives in rural Illinois. Over 350 of his tales and 100 of his poems have been published. His horror novel *Hawg* will be released Summer 2008 from Graveside Tales. His novel *Tormentor* will be released via Lachesis Publishing in May 2009. Visit him online at www.stevenshrewsbury.com

In all things, we should only be judged by our peers. –BALZAC, 1830

"I am sorry to trouble you with such a matter, Dr. Blackthorn," Edward Kilber said to me as we climbed out of his red Thunderbird.

"No problem, Ed," I told the man in his sixties. "I'm always willing to help another scientist at Miskatonic, even if I'm hauled out to Egypt, or in this case, Pocahontas County."

As I stood, stretched, and took in the tranquil scenery of the Allegheny Mountains that shrouded the small home, Dr. Kilber looked me over. "I also apologize that the front seat doesn't go back any farther."

"Not many archeologists are six foot ten, Ed. I'm pretty adaptable."

Ed soothed back his white hair. "I know a man of your talents, of psychometry and whatnot, may be able to crack this peculiar happening. It's not as exciting as the Droop Mountain battlefield stories, but it is different."

I shrugged and adjusted my thin leather gloves. My scuffed tan cowboy boots stepped onto the thriving grass that comes with spring in West Virginia. "Ed, I can see certain events in the past via my sense of touch. It doesn't work each time, but I'll give this deal a shot."

"That is all I can ask, Elijah."

A man looking like a youthful version of Dr. Kilber descended the steps of the home outside of Green Bank, West Virginia. I shook the hand of the man introduced to me as Patrick Kilber.

"Pleased to meet you, Dr. Blackthorn," Patrick said as he clasped my hand with firmness. Since I was so much larger than this man, he attempted to overcompensate his grip. He failed.

I nodded as my long black hair flew in the breeze. "Chilly for spring, no?"

Patrick frowned. "Chills me to the bone, Dr. Blackthorn. You don't see what I see every night. It's no Snedegar Poltergeist, but it will unnerve a fella."

Confused, my eyes narrowed at Patrick, but his father was quick to step forward. He said, "Elijah is the man from Miskatonic I told you about. He will be able to tell you more about the bones."

I folded my arms. "What I don't get is why you made such a discovery of bones and never contacted the authorities. If the find is deemed ancient, then I can help. The Bureau of Indian Affairs should be contacted, at least."

Patrick leered at me with green eyes smoking of hatred. "That's all you Indians want? Your land back."

"Patrick!" Ed shouted.

"Gonna build a casino in my back yard, Doc?" Patrick sneered. "You would, after I'm the only one near the Potomac Highlands with property that isn't vertical."

Ice fell from my words as I replied, "My Native American heritage has nothing to do with this, Pat. I'm probably full of more Caucasian blood than you. The law is the law. I will aide it or bend it slightly to help a friend, but the piper must be paid."

Patrick's teeth clenched, then snapped open long enough to say, "If this was a burial mound, then I lose my house? Freaking great! Just so you idiots can have a peace-pipe smoking ceremony?"

I sighed. "Your prejudice is like a pimple on an elephant's rear, Patrick. I came here because your father is a colleague." I think if I were a smaller man, Patrick would have hit me then. I went on. "He was concerned with these bones you have found on your property. Why you haven't reported them. . ."

"Patrick has a criminal record," Ed said.

"Dad," Patrick said, his look of anger transferring to his father.

"It was a minor thing," Dr. Kilber said. "One of his ex-girlfriends vanished when he was a teenager and the authorities in Stony Bottom tried to say he was responsible. Silly girl probably drowned in the Greenbrier River over that way. He had a long line of battery charges at the time, as a minor, of course."

Patrick said, "I was innocent."

"A minor thing by a minor?" I mused aloud. "So you thought he wouldn't want to draw attention to himself in such a way, reopen old wounds?"

Dr. Kilber smiled. "You are kind, Elijah."

Patrick blurted, "Screw the bones. What about the ghosts?"

My eyebrows must have fell to the ground. "Ghosts? I thought you were kidding and this was only about bones."

"Elijah, he has found these bones behind his house," Dr. Kilber said, "but it appears this new property is haunted."

"Such a thing is not my field, Ed. I deal in the past and events hidden there."

Dr. Kilber insisted, "Please, Elijah, touch the bones and tell me why these spirits torment my son."

I eyed Patrick, who seemed to be growing smaller and gravitating toward his home. "Who owned this house before you?"

Patrick waved at the acre of property secluded in the edge of the woods and said, "Some old dude. He died and an auction happened. I got it in a steal. I've been working steady at the National Radio Astronomy Observatory and this spot was the right price. I did some sleuthing myself, for your information, Dr. Blackthorn, and found the property had been in the oldster's family for a spell."

Dr. Kilber motioned for us to follow him behind the house. As we walked, I looked at a large area of the backyard covered in a green tarp. I stepped away from them and lifted up the edge of the covering. A large rectangular area of raw earth stared back at me, but no bones.

I asked, "Contact anyone concerning this find whatsoever?"

"How could I?" Patrick whispered and kicked a dirt-covered spade that lay beside the hole. The dirty shovel fell and twisted in the dirt. I dropped the tarp and followed the older man, never making eye contact with Patrick.

When Dr. Kilber slid open the door to the long machine shed and pointed at the series of skeletons laid out on a ping-pong table, I saw why.

"Infants," I stated the obvious as the workbench lights came on.

Patrick nodded. "Half dozen of them."

I almost added, You can count, but decided against it. "None are complete."

"I did the best I could!" Patrick said. "I was making a barbecue pit and kept finding bodies, so for all I know there are more out in my backyard."

The overhead light and the glow from the workbench shed enough illumination for me to declare, "They were all newborns. Look at the skulls. The tops are not even closing in. Hmm." I removed my gloves and took a deep breath. "So the ghosts are that of infants?"

"No, the ghosts are full grown," Patrick said, still fuming.

The idea of ghost-babies tiptoed across my brain at that moment, but I tried to stay focused. "Interesting. Do they come to you often?"

Patrick shrugged. "In the night or when I drink. Hey Doc, it ain't a hallucination. They are real as anything."

"The ghosts only showed up after the bones were disinterred?"

Patrick swallowed loud enough for me to hear it and Dr. Kilber nodded. That made me wonder, but I pocketed my gloves and flexed my hands. "I see."

"Any information will be of use," Ed told me.

"So no one misplaced a half dozen babies, huh, Patrick?"

"What do ya mean by that?"

"In your sleuthing, Patrick, surely you found out if anyone young enough to bear children lived here? It would be a terrible thing to have to live with tiny lives on one's mind."

"The old fossil who died here, his kid's family once lived here. They were Roman Catholic as the day is long. They had about a dozen kids, but none died that I saw."

I smiled and reached for the bones. "You'll have that in Catholic homes."

When I touched the bones, nothing happened at first. The gift or curse of psychometry can be an instant view of the past . . . a split second or a long look. Most of the time when I'm touching objects, weapons or tools, I see through the eyes of those who held such objects. In this case, I touched the bones of humanity itself. I wasn't sure if it would work, seeing as these people never lived long enough to walk.

My eyes blinked and a murky realm of shadows intermingled with emerald light rippled about my face. I saw a dim view of dirt shoveled over my eyes, then being surrounded by several adult people, all nude. They embraced me and stood in a circle. The area was the backyard of Patrick's house. They patted me on the back and welcomed me. A brown-haired man shoveled dirt on a spot in the back yard and fell to his knees. He made the sign of the cross and wept.

I saw the truth, that none of these infants was murdered, but drew but a single breath and died. It was natural and a part of the cycle of life. I blinked and stood in the shed with the two men, but we were no longer alone. The apparitions, the very souls of the infants walked out of the tiny bones before me. In moments, they grew into adults and pointed at Patrick.

Confused and afraid, I knew he had no role in their deaths, but why did they have a problem with him? Was he in their space? Was he disturbing their slumber in their bones?

As I realized Dr. Kilber and Patrick could see these billowy, white forms as well, suddenly from the ground, from the walls and from the ceiling sprouted shapes that are more translucent. These were almost subhuman creatures, but quickly transformed into infants. Patrick screamed and ran from the tool shed.

"Son," Ed shouted, but Patrick shook with horror and headed around the house.

I stepped outside and witnessed Patrick halt. An army of tiny infants marched like puppets, hobbling alone made him take pause. In their legion-like march, they scared Patrick enough to make him back up. Each baby started to grow larger and take on an adult form, all pointing. They called him by name, and they called him father.

Patrick turned and ran, crossing the backyard. In his terror, he fell into the large hole covered by the tarp. A single sharp scream and he lay still. The army of ghosts stopped, still and open-mouthed as if stunned.

I ran to the hole and pulled the tarpaulin away. The point of the spade had impaled Patrick Kilber just under his sternum, running him through to the backbone. He turned over slow and one breath escaped from him. A gory mass of blood and intestines then ejected out of him from the wound.

Dr. Kilber cried and fell to his knees. His weeping voice moaned across the mountains. All around me, the wraithlike images exchanged glances, smiled and vanished.

As I dialed my cell phone, Dr. Kilber asked, "Why, Elijah? Why did this happen to him?"

I called the police and paramedics, for all the good they could do. The idea of why was a complicated one and the answer would not be what Dr. Kilber wanted to hear.

"Ed," I said with a gentle tone. "We all have things we would rather forget. What did Patrick do to this girl when he was young?"

Dr. Kilber coughed, choked and said, "We will never know. I know she was blackmailing him, knowing I had money. He said he took care of the problem, but never told me how."

"Was she pregnant?"

He shook his head from side to side. "I don't know, Elijah. What are you saying?"

"I'm not sure," I said. But how could I tell him what I really thought? Were any of my suspicions valid?

"Patrick had no children?"

"No, I say." Ed wept. "He always had the girls, you know, get rid of them."

I put my gloves back on. Did Patrick's progeny come back for revenge? Did they plot with others who never walked in flesh? The thought of such a conspiracy in the nether-realm made my heart race.

It also made me make a note to hug my son Jakob when I went home. Tight.

Occurrence at Flatwoods

Michael Laimo

Michael Laimo has written the novels *Fires Rising, Dead Souls, Atmosphere, Deep In the Darkness, The Demonologist,* and *Sleepwalker.* His short stories have been collected in *Dark Ride, Demons, Freaks, and Other Abnormalities,* and *Dregs of Society.* He's recently completed another horror novel and is currently working on a thriller. Visit him at myspace.com/michaellaimo.

I'm in a room. A hospital room? Peering peripherally through the tender, swollen slits of my eyes, I see IV bags—a few of them on both sides of me—hanging from poles, clear plastic tubes snaking into my wrists, my arms, liquid trickling within. I attempt to move but feel only the burning agony of my skin, red and inflamed from head to toe: a blanket of open sores. My throat is on fire, barely able to aid in my labored breathing. And all I remember is vomiting—how it rolled out of my mouth ungoverned—and the hands that appeared from the blur that surrounds me, holding instruments to suck it all up.

This is all I know.

But soon, I fall asleep, and remember in my dreams how I got here.

***

"They went that way, Sheriff." The woman was crying, lips trembling, wet with spit and tears. I peered toward the woods but saw only blackness in the play of my flashlight, tree boughs groaning in the wind, wet leaves rustling in their ceaseless sway.

Donna Nutley had two boys, ages fifteen and twelve. Evidently they'd gone off into the woods to investigate a loud booming noise, and had not returned. The family mutt had gone with them, and Donna claimed to hear its exploratory barking for about ten minutes before it yelped once in the distance, and went silent.

"You stay here, Ma'am." I nodded once to Donna, noting her tears and how they'd carved swaths through her makeup. "I'll find your boys."

I'd had it in my right mind to check her breath for whiskey. A lot of folks here in Flatwoods, much less all of Braxton County, have not much more to do than spend their free time at the local taverns, making love to the spirits. In a frantic voice, she'd called my office and claimed that after hearing the booming noise, It sounded like a bomb went off, I'm telling ya, Sheriff, the power had gone out in her house, and that the house itself trembled as if there were an earthquake. It rattled the trivets on the wall in the kitchen!

A thirty-second check with the state police revealed no such phenomena in the area—no earthquakes or power outages had been reported. Still, her boys were gone, going on a whole hour now, and for Donna Nutley, that was reason enough to investigate.

I paced across the backyard toward the woods surrounding her home, feet squelching in the wet grass. Braxton County is made up of forests, nearly seventy-five percent of the land untouched by man. The hunting is good in the fall, but here in the spring the rains pretty much saturate everything in its wake, making the area good for nothing but mosquito mating, which is good for pheasant feeding, which is good for hunting in the fall.

I'd planned accordingly, wearing rubber boots just for the occasion. Good thing I did; I was ankle deep in mud three minutes into my walk.

I aimed the flashlight over the trees and the sodden path, the boys' footsteps clearly visible as I ventured deeper. Moonlight trickled in through the moving canopy, scattering hints of blue across the trees like ghosts. I called out for the boys, "Neil? Ronnie?" but there was no answer. All I had was their tracks, which led deeper into the woodland.

It stood to reason that the two teenagers were looking for an excuse to get out of their mother's way, to take a smoke in the woods perhaps—most of the kids in Flatwoods try it sooner or later anyway. I suppose I prefer they do that than drink. As long as they stay out of trouble, I think parents shouldn't make a big deal of it.

About a quarter-mile in, the land inclined sharply into a hill. The boy's tracks, still visible in the mud, arched up and over the hill, where a clearing in the trees opened. I climbed the hill carefully, staggering a bit and unable to keep the flashlight pointed ahead as I gathered my balance. My footsteps sunk real deep into the mud . . . or what appeared to be two elongated tracks in the mud that went up and over the top of the hill.

Finally reaching top, winded from the exertion and gasping for air, I looked down at my boots. In the flashlight's beam I saw not mud, but a black tar-like substance that'd oozed jellyfish-like over my ankles, all the way to the top of my boots. I used my heels to scrape some of it away, disgusted at the smell of it, then looked ahead.

The top of the hill was flat, sparse with trees and fairly bright with cold blue moonlight. The first thing that hit me as I stepped onto the clearing was the stench, a lot more of what I'd just smelled: a sickening burnt metallic odor, not too far off from the stink I'd experienced during my one and only visit to the steel mill at the outskirts of Braxton County.

My heart roared as I looked ahead.

There was something in the middle of the clearing.

I didn't see much more than a shadow at first. It had been dark, my flashlight's wavering beam picking up only the commonplace trees and copses. This led me to believe, at first, that I was looking at the dead husk of a tree trunk. But then, from out of nowhere it seemed, a red light began to glow right in the middle of the clearing.

In its faint splay, I saw the boys. Then the dog. Then it.

The boys and the dog were on the forest floor, seemingly stuck in the black stuff, which coated the entire hilltop and amassed upon the kids and their pet like an oil spill on snared gulls. They were covered in it, only slight patches of white skin and the whites of their unblinking eyes visible in the dark.

"Neil? Ronnie?" I called weakly.

No response. The three bodies . . . they were unmoving, frozen in time, as if in catatonic-like states, mannequins unable to move, much less whisper their fear of the thing that held them captive.

I should've pulled my gun at this moment. Should have pointed it. Should have pulled the trigger. But I couldn't. I was a captive now, a prisoner of my own sudden terror.

Of the monster standing before me.

It was at least ten feet tall, a thing human in form, but no more human than the dog it had captured. Its body was dark green, covered in scales that flared into a skirt shape from which two clawed feet emerged. I could see the razor-like talons of its feet, like those of an owl, holding down the two boys and the dog as it remained perched upon their prone bodies.

The red light it emitted came from its face—not from its eyes, which bulged whitely and obscenely from within the light—but from the face of the creature itself, an inverted heart shape, something like an ace-of-spades. It had no arms I could see, and judging from the appearance of its taloned feet, I wondered if it had wings instead, pressed tightly against its body like some great bird of prey.

I pulled my gun, palm wet against the grip. I should've run at this point, turned away from the thing and the boys, fled back through the woods all the way back to Donna Nutley's house. But I couldn't. My fear was calling the shots, and the first thing it shouted was Defend yourself! I pointed the gun at the thing—or close to it anyway, my hand was shaking so much—and managed to shout "Hey!" before the creature produced a shrill hissing noise that pierced my ears like a siren's blast.

I cowered, and fired my gun into the air. From a nearby oak tree, two more red lights blared, two more loud hisses. I bulleted my gaze in that direction, and saw within the lights two more creatures, just like the first.

I staggered back, feet slipping and skidding in the black gunk, and fell down onto my back. The creature before me, red face still aglow, floated into the air like a rising balloon, taking with it the two boys, their bodies dangling lifelessly from its clutching claws as it disappeared into the night sky. From the oak tree, the two other creatures took off, again not flying but gliding across the clearing as though propelled by something entirely mechanical. One sailed over the dog, picked it up with its feet, and sailed off after the first.

The third creature came at me. Without any further hesitation, I shot it, firing from my back into the air, piercing it in the chest as it plunged down at me. It emitted a red mist that seemed to materialize from the red light surrounding it (or was this its blood?). The mist settled down on me, all around me, burning my skin like acid from head to toe, right through my clothes.

I had not a second to scream before the thing landed on me, grasped me with its clawed feet, and took me up and away into the deep, dark night.

I awake from my dream . . . but not a dream at all. It's all real . . . until the images fade from my mind and I'm once again devoid of memories, lying here in this bed alongside the IVs that drip their clear contents into my veins.

The blur that surrounds me has cleared a bit. Perhaps I am healing now, my immune system fighting off the ill effects of the creature's mist. The Flatwoods Monster my mind tells me in a sudden recollection of the Mountain State legend. My God, the legend . . . it's true. The monster exists. It's returned to the Braxton County woodlands.

The blur clears a bit more. I can see others in the room with me now. Although I still can't see the walls that surround me, I do see three other dark forms here, also lying in beds, their IV stands coming into view like trees in a forest fog.

I squeeze my eyes shut. When I open them, I can see the bodies more clearly. There are three in all, the first two naked, the IV tubes running from a multitude of stands into the arms, their wrists . . . oh my god . . . their legs, their noses, and . . . and into the groins of the two boys. Neil and Ronnie Nutley.

The third body comes into clear view now. It's the dog. It too is laying on a bed . . . but not really a bed, I can see now. Like the boys, the dog is lying atop a steel table, body pierced by a dozen or more tubes. It's here that I realize with dread: some of the tubes aren't feeding clear liquids into it. They're filled with red, yellow, and white fluids: they're drawing out the dog's blood. Its urine. And God knows what else.

I start to panic, manage to thump my body on the bed—not a bed, but a steel table. . .

Soon, from the fading blur, the hands appear at my sides.

Not hands.

Claws.

The clawed feet of the Flatwoods monsters. As they adjust the IV bags, as the tubes fill up with a colorful mixture of my bodily fluids, I recall the legend of Braxton County, and realize now that I'm in no hospital ward.

That the creatures are not borne of this earth.

The memories of my night in the woods behind the home of Donna Nutley fade into nothingness . . . everything is gone.

Everything except the creature, the alien, and how it lifted me off into the night sky, to its waiting ship.

A House is Not a Home

Maurice Broaddus

Maurice Broaddus is a writer, scientist, and lay leader at The Dwelling Place Church. He's been published in dozens of markets, including *Apex SF* and *Horror Digest, Horror Literature Quarterly*, and *Weird Tales*. Learn more about him and read his blog at www.MauriceBroaddus.com.

Preston Matthews climbed out of the car and felt every bit the trespasser. The full moon bathed the yard in pale light and threw the house into a foreboding relief. Thin blades of grass protruded through the cracks of the concrete slab in the middle of the small yard.

"A carriage house originally stood there," Sakineh Obaob said. "I bet it had stone around its base, too, to echo the house."

"Someone probably stole it."

"It's not much to look at, I know," she said, "but you have to have vision."

The city of Ceredo offered many quaint homes with interesting architecture, and varying states of disrepair, far from the cookie-cutter neighborhood where they currently lived. The trim was painted a muted brown in forlorn contrast to the dull green of the rest of the house.

"Mama always said be wary of homes with their own names."

"Really? Is that was mama said? Ransdell House doesn't exactly ring with terror. Besides, you know what they say—you visit a house during the day to see what the realtor wants to show you and at night to see what they don't want you to see." Sakineh pressed her petite frame alongside him, coaxing a begrudging squeeze out of him. Her features were exquisite and delicate: lips painted too red for her face, wide brown eyes that took in as much of life as they could.

"Really? Is that what they say?" Preston's heart wasn't in his reflexive sarcasm. She'd already won him over.

"You just have to look beyond the . . . old. Plus, he only wants thirty thousand."

"How do you know?"

"I asked him."

"There's not even a for sale sign up."

"Just because there's no for sale sign doesn't mean it's not for sale. I asked a realtor, he asked the owner."

"The same realtor that's supposed to be meeting us." Preston stared at her with justifiably skeptical eyes. He was familiar with the coming song and dance. They were both artists, Preston a musician and Sakineh a painter, so they understood the need for impulse in the creative instinct and process.

"Yes. No. I picked up the keys this morning. Come on. You'll just love the living room."

"You've already been in."

"No. Yes. Last week, when I first saw the place."

"You mean, when you drove by?"

"I couldn't wait."

"You broke in?"

"Does it look like anyone lives here? Or cares?"

"This is supposed to encourage me to buy? The house has already driven my wife to B & E while my would-be apathetic neighbors look on."

"C'mon, you'll love it as much as I do." Her perkiness bordered on abusive.

They strode the length of the stone-wrapped porch and slipped past the dripping water from the leaf-clogged guttering. Old paint chipped from the house like a teen with bad eczema. Preston wondered how many pencils he could fashion from all the lead in the old paint.

"Luckily, it was built to last. They don't make 'em like this anymore."

"They couldn't afford it. That's a 15 to 20 thousand dollar roof job."

"See, you can't wait either." Sakineh, much more in the spirit of things, made quite the production of finding the right key. Subtle she was not: big house, lots of locks, lots of keys, lots of mystery. When she found the right key and opened the door, it only swung about a foot before it jammed on swollen tiles. "We can fix that."

A mound of envelopes climbed toward the mail slot of the side door. Many of the letters had molded together into a single, fibrous paper tumor. Preston flipped through the loose ones, ignoring his internal alarm at the impropriety of treading on the ghosts of occupants past. Rarely were any two envelopes addressed to the same person: mostly bills, the occasional summons, a few government agencies in search of people in order to justify their existence. Ransdell House had been many things to many people over the years. He could taste the mold in the air. Black spots peppered the peeling wallpaper like liver warts. Black cracks veined the exposed plaster of the walls. They walked around the large living room that ran the length of the house. Pocket doors would have broken the room were they not permanently stuck in their coves. One of the rooms would make the perfect studio. Moonlight poured in at odd angles from the windows, but with so many odd nooks and crannies, the shadows created pockets of sadness, isolation, darkness. The stairwell wound into the upper shadows.

"Why is there a bathroom in the living room?" Preston asked.

"It's not in the living room, it's off the living room. Look at the wall line," Sakineh pointed. "It's not supposed to be here."

"Someone came along and decided that the middle of our living room could be a good place for a toilet."

"Our living room?" Sakineh smiled.

"Big picture, honey, stay with me. Toilet."

"When I talked to the realtor, he said, off the record, that Ransdell House used to be a stop on the Underground Railroad."

"I bet every house up for sale makes that same claim, honey. History jacks up the price."

"It's supposed to be haunted."

"Really? By who?"

"Slaves and stuff."

"Now we're talking. Think the owner would come down on the price? I mean, if we have to deal with unwanted co-tenants. . ."

Sakineh punched him lightly on his arm. "This is fun, in a forbidden sort of way."

"What? Exploring without someone's permission?"

"Come on. You've got to see upstairs."

The stairs smelled of urine, a DMZ where homeless waste met the methhead shooting gallery. The master bathroom, its thick, cast-iron tub with claw feet squatting in its center, overlooked the back yard and the alleyway.   Two bedrooms faced the front of the house, the third room, off to itself, faced the bedroom window of the neighboring house. Though it led out onto its own balconied porch and would catch the sun each day, the room was grey. Heartbreak hung in it like the memory of a child's death.

"We could make cathedral ceilings in our bedroom. And look at that molding."

"Look at that mold."

"We can antique together for Victorian furniture." She twirled her arms in a spinning dance of bliss. "You know, period pieces."

"Because it's always been my dream to fill my home with uncomfortable museum pieces." Even as he said it, Preston couldn't imagine their stainless steel appliances or modern furniture in this place. They now seemed so passionless and sterile.

"Think of how much of this we can do together. Can't you just see us wallpapering, painting and having paint fights, truly gutting this place."

"I don't know. A house like this needs to be restored. This history alone demands—" Preston found himself caressing the intricate woodwork of the banister as they retreated to the top of the stairs. Plaster had fallen free from several spots along the wall, the exposed lathe like the emaciated ribs of the house. "—respect."

"Or." Sakineh pressed close to him. "We could start from scratch and make this place our own. New couple, new history. We could spend a month 'initiating' each room."

Preston knew she wanted a child even more than he did, but years of trying had proven fruitless. Maybe a new beginning was what they needed.

"You make a fine argument, Sak. The roof's fine. Foundation's solid. As long as you're not looking for any casual amenities like air-conditioning, copper plumbing, wiring that's not . . . oh my God. It's cloth wiring . . . patched into newer stuff."

"We can fix that."

"Yes. I suppose we can."

Sakineh pulled away from him. "Did you hear that?"

Preston cocked his head, sorting the silence. A susurrus of whispers accompanied a dim scraping. A wan light flickered to life, illuminating the outline of a doorway along the ceiling, an attic perhaps. Meth heads probably broke in to get high. Preston and Sakineh lingered momentarily, paralyzed by indecision mixed with curiosity. The light snuffed abruptly. He pressed his finger to his lips, took her by her hand, and they backed unsteadily down the stairs. The scrape returned, slithering from the depths of the murky darkness, slowly resolving itself into the sounds of clanking chains. Metal strained against metal, faint at first, then growing ever louder, like shackled arms flailing in the night slowly gaining their strength.

They skittered down the steps, desperate to re-trace their steps but getting turned about in the gloom. A series of rooms ran parallel to the long living room as they wound through the house. The tile wainscot rose high along the wall of the dining room, the hand-drawn floral bouquet wall treatment above it, too much an estranged affectation. The further back they ran, the more the house recalled a stirred vitality, as if it remembered days past.

The corridor slimmed. Preston realized they had wandered into the pantry. His fingers scrabbled for the doorknob he sensed led to the kitchen and an exit. Heavy footfalls, like soldiers' boots, tromped along the floorboards above them, stopping and resuming their pacing as if searching for something. Or someone.

Preston's hand shook as he latched onto the recessed, almost hidden, handle. They tumbled into the waiting maw of darkness. The wall of spider silk they brushed through informed him of his miscalculation. Sakineh stifled a startled yelp. The basement steps strained with a dull groan under their weight. He turned to return the way they came, but the steady tramping of boots patrolled right outside the concealed door. Preston and Sakineh retreated further into the darkness.

The basement walls seemed carved out of the earth itself, dredged clay and clotted material forming the walls. Sakineh's hand tightened on his. He felt the sudden presence of others. They kept moving closer, shadows in the night, quiet but pressing ever nearer. Preston had trouble breathing as the bodies huddled against him. Some shivered—despite the warmth of mashed bodies crammed into the aperture—weak with sickness, judging from their thick sweat and muffled coughs. Flies circled the piles of waste buried in corners, the smell of stale urine assailed his nostrils. Preston dry-heaved, though his empty belly had nothing to recall, his body contented itself with heady waves of nausea. His eyes had not adjusted to the deepened darkness; he knew only that dozens of people lined that passage with him. The temperature climbed steadily in the crush of bodies. An elbow poked into his gut. The air soured as they breathed the desperate gulps of their neighbor's exhalations. A knee found purchase in his groin as the owner jostled for position. Muffled cries haunted the darkness. Slowly shuffling forward, they squeezed past other sweaty bodies, in small steps toward freedom.

The suffocating smell of unwashed bodies, the thick and gamey body odor of field workers, coated his throat. The pressure to scream built in his chest. To just cry out, if only to be heard, to release the pent-up terror. Flies buzzed in his ears, about his face, with him unable to shoo them off because of his pinned arms. The occasional scrape of metal against stone, or echoing jangle of a loose chain managed to cut through the expectant din of murmurs. The steps became fewer. More and more of us crammed into the small space. Preston struggled for each breath of fouled air.

Preston spied a lookout window along the top of the basement. He lifted Sakineh, holding her steady against the bodies smashed against him, hot, moist, clinging. Weak arms grappled at him as if not wanting them to escape. Or, rather, draw notice to them. Sakineh crawled out of the window, with Preston following, and they ran into the night.

That night, from the security of his own bed, Preston dreamed of chains and darkness.

Dark Wisdom

Gary A. Braunbeck

Gary A. Braunbeck is the author of 10 novels and nine short story collections, one non-fiction memoir, and has edited two anthologies. His work has garnered five Bram Stoker Awards, an International Horror Guild Award, three *Shocklines* "Shocker" Awards, and a Black Quill Award from *Dark Scribe Magazine*. To learn more about Gary and his work, please visit www.garybraunbeck.com.

He was sleeping in his truck about half a block from the grade school, hidden in the shadows of 2 A.M. autumn in this neighborhood where the cops don't patrol like they ought to; all I had to do was yank open the door, pull him out, and slam the butt of the 9mm hard against his mouth a few times until I felt the blood on my hands, and then when he started to cuss me I pistol-whipped the side of his head until he either lost consciousness or maybe decided that it was best to keep his opinions to himself, just to be polite.

I knelt down and slung him over my shoulder, carrying him to my van. Ain't too many men in the their 70s what can say they can carry the weight of a younger man on their backs—especially one as fat as him—but I been keeping myself in good condition ever since the days at Moundsville, and was always grateful that I got out of that crap-hole of a prison alive and in one piece. After that last riot in 1986 (I was three years gone by then, thank goodness), it was a wonder anybody got out alive. I know of several guys who didn't make it out in one piece when the place was finally shut down in '95, the West Virginia Supreme Court being the bunch of get-right-on-it go-getters they are.

I tossed him into the back of my van and then climbed in, closing the door and reaching for the rope. I resisted the urge to hog-tie him on account of seeing one story too many on the news about cops who hog-tie a prisoner, only to have the poor S.O.B. choke to death or suffocate. I wanted him alive and kicking.

I debated a moment about putting a gag on him, but as soon as he started to come to from the pistol-whipping, he started in again with cussing the likes of which I hadn't heard since my prison days, and since that kind of language didn't exactly get me to feeling all nostalgic, I shoved a wadded-up section of cloth in his mouth.

"If you want me to take that out, son," I said, "then you talk to me respectful, understand?"

His eyes let me know that wasn't gonna happen anytime soon, so I just left things as they were.

I climbed into the driver's seat. "In case you're wondering where I'm taking you, that's just too bad. But if you wanna know why I'm doing this, then I got a name for you: Todd Barnes." I put the van in gear.

"You look through that swamp of a mind of yours and see if you don't remember him . . . or any of them other kids and what you done to them."

I looked at the file on the seat next to me and had to fight to keep from getting sick. I knew every face and newspaper story in there by heart. I hadn't had a decent night's sleep in darn near two years on account of what this fat moron had been up to. My hope was that I'd sleep better come this time tomorrow night.

He started thrashing around in the back. I turned around and shoved the business end of the 9mm right against his forehead.

"You best behave yourself, son, or I swear that I will put a bullet through each of your kneecaps, and it's my understanding that that hurts considerable. Don't think I got any compunctions about doing it, neither. Don't matter to me if you're in pain when we get to where we're heading, just so long as you're alive and conscious."

He stared at me and must've seen in my eyes that I meant business, 'cause the next thing I know his eyes get all teary like he's gonna start bawling like a baby. He gave a slow nod of his head and then rolled onto his side, real still-like.

"That's my boy," I said, driving away.

***

The Moundsville State Penitentiary was always a creepy place, even when it was open and filled to busting with some of the most violent, depraved, and . . . well, not particularly nice inmates. Driving up to it now under the glow of a sick-seeming moon, it looked as if the darn thing had actually grown since the last time I'd been here. But, then, I suppose that's what cancer growths do.

"Hey," I called over my shoulder. "Did you know that Charles Laughton filmed some exteriors for *The Night of the Hunter* at the Moundsville Penn? You ever see that? Robert Mitchum was crazy in that movie."

I'd left the gate open so I wouldn't have to get out of the van and leave him alone. I drove through and into the yard.

"It's no wonder," I said, "all of them ghost hunters come here. Place always did look like something out of a Boris Karloff movie. And you got yourself an honest-to-Pete Indian burial ground not too far from here." I was talking because the silence of this place gave me the willies. It wasn't just that there was silence, understand; it was like there was something in here that sucked all of the sound and energy from the air, greedy-like, always hungry, always chewing and swallowing and sometimes spitting out the pieces that weren't to its liking. And now it's a tourist attraction. People came from all over the country to tour the place and get video of them standing by or sitting in Old Sparky. I will never understand how a sane human being could get a thrill out of being in a place where so many men died, and some of them deaths not so neat and tidy. Glorious species we are sometimes.

I parked in front of the door I needed, and then removed the syringe from where I'd taped it inside the file.

"You don't give me no trouble here, son," I said, climbing in the back with him. I had the syringe in one hand, the 9mm in the other. "That whole kneecap thing still applies."

He didn't make any noise, didn't thrash around, didn't try kneeing me in the groin; at least he was smart enough to know there was no way he could fight back. I pulled back one of his sleeves and inserted the needle. "You have yourself a little nap now." And sank the plunger.

***

When he came around about fifteen minutes later, I'd already cuffed him to the chain I'd strung around one of the sturdier overhead pipes in the basement. The bright light from a battery-operated lantern held us in the perimeter of its twenty-foot glow.

I'd also removed his shoes, socks, pants, and underwear. I imagine the stone floor felt a tad cold against his bare rear-end, judging from the way he immediately started scooting around, trying to get to his feet.

"I'd save my strength, if I was you," I said. "I greased the bottoms of your feet. No way you're getting up under your own power. Do you have any idea where we are?"

He shook his head.

"This is what used to be called The Sugar Shack back in the days when I was still a guard here. It was intended to be a secondary exercise yard for the inmates when the outside weather got too nasty."

I knelt down a few feet away from him, pointing the 9mm at his midsection. "At first, there used to be several guards down here with them, then, after a while, only a few guards. It finally got to the point where a group of guards would lead whichever cellblock's turn it was down here, and then close and lock the door with no guards inside and only one posted out in the hall.

"Nobody ever died or was killed in here, but there was quite a number of inmates what died from their injuries gotten in this place. And most of them got injured because they fought back at the Sugar Dads. Not a good idea."

He made a small noise. His eyes got this pleading look in them.

"You wanna talk, is that it?"

He nodded his head, looking for all the world like one of them stupid bobble-head figures you see on some peoples' dashboards when they pass you in traffic.

I started to reach for the makeshift gag I'd stuffed in his mouth, then paused. "Two things, son. One—you start in with all that cussing again, and the wad goes back in your mouth. Two—if you bite my fingers when I take that out, I'll shoot. Nod if this has sunk in far enough."

He nodded. Once.

I pulled the wad of cloth from his mouth.

"Dad, please," he cried. "Please don't do this."

"I never thought I'd hear these words coming out of my mouth," I said, "but I am so glad that your mother didn't live to see what her 'best little boy in the world' turned into. It would've killed her, and then you'd have two deaths on your hands right now."

"Hey, I didn't kill any of them kids, not a one. That Todd Barnes, he was alive when I dumped him off."

"There's alive, and then there's surviving." I reached into the file folder and pulled out Barnes's picture. "You take a good look at his face, you piece of crap. You had him for five days when he was nine years old. You know what happened just this morning? What should have been the morning of his eleventh birthday?

"He hanged himself. Imagine—his parents come sneaking upstairs to give him a surprise birthday breakfast in bed, and they find him dangling from one of the ceiling beams in his room. Not even a dozen years on this earth, and you gave him such a bellyful of sickness and shame and hurt that it would've been a mercy if you had killed him. He was already dead before you dumped him in the middle of downtown."

His eyes went cold and his features relaxed. "Like I said. I didn't kill him."

"That help you sleep better nights? Knowing that even though you tortured and raped a little boy, his death ain't on your hands?"

His expression changed when I said "tortured and raped." He looked downright nostalgic.

"Don't knock it until you've tried it."

It took everything I had not to shoot him in the knees; instead, I picked up the folder and scattered its contents all over the floor in front of him. "Thirteen children in the past two years, all of them taken from a public place by you and then . . . you know what you done to 'em before dumping them off."

"How'd you figure out it was me?"

"Aside from all of the kids' descriptions of you matching almost exactly, right down to that long scar you got from belly to groin from where your spleen burst when you was a kid? I figured it out a long time ago, but then you went and confirmed my suspicions. The last little girl you took from White Lakes Mall. You got sloppy. They got you on tape this time. No one's identified you yet, but the minute that picture come up on the television screen, I recognized you right away. A parent always knows their child."

Behind us, deep in the dank bottomless shadows of the Sugar Shack, a low and guttural sound began to take shape, growing in volume until it became the cumulative groan of a hundred starving men crawling toward a banquet table.

"Wh-what's that?" he asked.

"Not just yet," I replied. "You—hey, boy, you look at me when I'm talking to you. That's better." I moved toward him, knelt down, and pressed the business end of the 9mm against his groin. "How many have there been? My count's thirteen."

"Why do you want to know?"

"Because I need to know how many of your twisted sins I have to atone for in the eyes of God. Weren't for me and my seed, you'd never been a part of this world, and all of them kids, they'd be happy and healthy and alive. They wouldn't be on medicine to keep the nightmares away. They wouldn't be so changed that there's no making them right again. They'd not have the kind of dark wisdom you gave to them."

The sound was getting louder. I turned around, grabbed up the lantern, turned it in the direction of the shadows, and there they were. The Sugar Dads.

There might have been fifty of them, there might have been a couple of hundred, it was hard to tell, what with the way they kept moving in and out of the blackness; but a glimpse at any one of their faces and you'd know they were not going to be anything like Casper, the Friendly Ghost.

I used to think that hauntings had little to do with a ghost trying to finish something left behind. I always thought that hauntings had everything to do with sorrow and regret. But down here in the basement, in the crypt of the Sugar Shack, one look at any of the Sugar Dads and I knew what hauntings had everything to do with: hunger.

One of them moved out of the shadows to give us a better look. This one still wore its prisoner uniform—I suspected they'd all be dressed in them—and it looked as fresh and clean as they day it had first been put on. Too bad you couldn't say that about the thing wearing it.

Skeletal hands covered in a discolored, paper-thin film that had once been skin, both hands opening and then closing fists, impatient for the banquet to begin. Its head was smooth and bald. Its face was at least three times as long as a normal human face, its mouth a great, gaping insect maw, slowly opening, drooling, and then closing as its raw-liver tongue licked its lips. Its eyes were twice as big as they should have been, and were little more than two oversized black marbles, and the flesh of its face was loose, hanging jowl-like all over, fishbelly-slick and the grey pallor of rotted meat.

I heard the sounds behind me and turned to see what was going on.

He'd scooted himself as far back and away from me and the ghost of the Sugar Dad as he could get, but the chain stopped him from getting any farther than he was right now. His eyes were wide with panic, and when he spoke his voice was a long, grating whine.

"Oh god, please—please, Dad, don't do this to me! Listen, listen, I'll . . . I'll turn myself in, okay? You can gather up all these photos and stuff and you can give me another shot and take me to the police and turn me in. It don't need to be this way, Dad, please?"

"Yes, it does," I said. "Don't get me wrong, boy, I got every intention of turning you in. If you're still alive come sunup."

Behind me, the Sugar Daddies were gathering in a large circle. It occurred to me as I looked at them that each one was twisted and deformed in their own unique way, yet the faces were all exactly alike. I wondered if maybe what I was seeing was the true shape of their souls. Then decided it didn't matter.

I started toward the doorway.

"Dad, please! This isn't . . . isn't fair!"

I almost laughed at that, but I felt like I was either going to vomit or weep at any given second. I watched a pair of the Sugar Daddies roll the thing that was once my son over onto his stomach. I didn't need to see what was about to happen.

I all but ran out of there and up the stairs. Once out in the yard, I pressed my back to the wall and didn't so much sit as I did slide down to the ground. The stars were out in full force tonight, blinking down from the depths of a cold, indifferent Heaven like they knew some big secret they weren't about to let you in on.

I pulled out the flask of Jack Daniels and my pack of smokes, settling in for a long night. The stars kept winking at me. The night breeze was cool and sharp. The place was quiet, empty-feeling. I leaned my head back and listened to the echoes of the screams coming from down in the bowels of the building.

They were a lullaby to my ears. I was asleep in five minutes.

An Angel in the Balcony

Brian J. Hatcher

Brian J. Hatcher is a writer and poet living in Charleston WV. When asked if he believes in ghosts, Brian will often smile, knowingly. He does confirm the clock incident described in this short story is true. When it happened, he was the actor on stage. Visit Brian online at www.brianjhatcher.com.

Denise stood center stage in the Capitol Plaza Theater, feeling nothing at all like a star. Come Friday she would be, but to what degree she didn't care to guess. As Denise looked out at the empty seats, her modesty wouldn't allow her to imagine a full house. She'd be grateful for any filled seat, and if she could send the audience home entertained and moved, it would be good enough.

Suddenly, the sound of clapping rang out from the darkened house. Rich applauded as he walked down the aisle. "Bravo! Bravo!"

As always, he could make Denise smile in spite of herself. "Wise guy."

"Just getting you ready for Friday night."

Denise descended the stairs at the side of the apron, and went into the house. "I thought you wanted to wait for me in the car."

"And I thought you were just running in to get the key."

Denise looked at her watch. "I'm sorry. I didn't realize I'd been gone that long. I just wanted to take a look around."

"I can see why," Rich said. "This theater is something else."

"You've never been here before?"

"I didn't go to plays until after we started dating. I must have driven past this theater a thousand times, but never really noticed it."

"Most people don't. The Capitol Plaza's been a part of downtown Charleston for over a century. We take it for granted."

"It's kind of creepy, being in here by ourselves. I can see why people say the place is haunted."

"Says who?"

Rich shrugged. "I've heard stories."

"Like what?"

"Well, a friend of mine told me that back in the early '90s the University of Charleston put on a play here. It was one of the first plays performed in this theater after the renovations.

"There's this scene where the main character decides to hang himself. The actor wraps a rope around his neck, and the lights go out.

"Just then, a clock on the desk starts chiming. Thing is, the clock isn't supposed to chime. It's not even wound; it's just set dressing. But it still chimes.

"The actor on stage, the actors backstage, even the people in the audience hear it. Twelve, thirteen, fourteen times, the clock keeps chiming.

"Then, as the lights go up, suddenly the clock stops."

"Are you serious?" Denise asked.

"The guy who told me this said he was in the audience. Swears it happened."

"Wow," Denise said. "I had no idea the Capitol Plaza had a ghost."

"Two, actually. John Welch, the guy who owned the mansion that used to stand here, and Molly Welch, his daughter."

Denise laughed. "You seem to know a lot about this. You never told me you were a Ghostbuster."

"Hardly. But I grew up reading *Coffin Hollow* and *The Telltale Lilac Bush* like a lot of kids. I really got into them. Local ghost stories became a hobby of mine. Look, I'm not saying ghosts are real, or that they're not. But they do make great stories. I'm not spooking you out, am I?"

"Of course not. You know I'm not superstitious."

Rich laughed. "Please. Actors are the most superstitious people I know."

"Not me. Complete skeptic."

"Really? Well, then you won't mind my saying the name of, what is that Shakespeare play?"

"Don't you dare!"

"Yeah, the Bloody Scott's play, with the witches. Starts with an M—"

Denise punched Rich in the arm. "You do it, and I'll kill you."

"Ow!" Rich rubbed his arm. "I thought you weren't superstitious."

"Like I said, complete skeptic. But why push my luck?"

"Denise, honey," Tammy called out from the house, "put your hand down. I can't tell if the lights are hitting your face."

"Trust me, they're hitting it," Denise said. She'd been onstage tuning up the light cues for an hour, and the lights were killing her eyes. Tammy was a good director—and a great friend—but she could be a real slave driver during a show, especially on tech week.

"Take a step forward," Tammy said. "How's she look, Kev?"

Tammy had brought Kevin in as lighting director. "She's too toplit. I can't see her face."

"Can we focus the cans farther downstage?" Tammy asked.

"We need those lights for Scene 2. But I do have that spot focused there. Let me try using that to fill her in." The stage lights dimmed, and Kevin punched up the spot.

"She's washed out," Tammy said.

"Give me a minute; I need to dim the spot. Let me know when the level's where you want it."

The spot slowly dimmed. "Right there," Tammy said. "Perfect."

"I'll program it in," Kevin said. "Any other light cues you need fixed."

"That should do it. Do you need another run-through?"

Denise tried not to groan too loudly. It was already past midnight.

"No," Kevin said, "I got it. Unless there's something you need to go over?"

"No, I think we have it. See you tomorrow. Denise, come on down for notes."

Denise went into the house and took a seat next to Tammy. "All right, lay it on me."

Tammy looked over her clipboard. "Not much to say. The show's coming together. But it wouldn't be rehearsal if I didn't give you 'the note'."

Denise sighed. "I know. I always screw up that last monologue."

"It's not that you're screwing it up," Tammy said. "Your problem is you have to put away your writer's cap and be an actor."

"Maybe we should cut the scene."

"Trust me, you want to leave it in."

"I don't know," Denise said. "Maybe we should have gotten another actor."

"Honey, how long have you been in theater?"

"I don't know. I started doing tech for Light Opera Guild about the time Jennifer Garner left for New York."

"Okay, let's just say you've been doing this a while. I've seen you perform. If anyone could get away with writing and performing a one-woman show, it's you. Just don't get so hung up on trying to wring emotion out of that last scene. Just live in the moment, and whatever emotions come out will be perfect, because they'll be real."

"I'll try."

Tammy hugged her. "You really do have a great show. And you're going to wow them tomorrow." Tammy got her clipboard and headed for the aisle. "You need a ride home?"

"I have my car. I just want to sit here awhile. Get my head straight for tomorrow."

"You okay?"

"Sure. Not even the ghosts could keep me away."

"What?" Tammy asked.

"Oh, nothing. My boyfriend told me a story yesterday about how there's supposed to be ghosts in this theater."

"You mean John and Molly Welch?"

"You know about that?"

"Of course. John's a bit of a prankster, but he's very protective of the actors on stage. His daughter Molly died of pneumonia when she was eight years old. Some people say you sometimes see her sitting in the balcony."

"Well, nobody's watching the show without paying, ghost or not."

Tammy shook her head. "At least your sense of humor is coming back. Are you sure you're okay?"

"Yeah, I'm fine."

"Okay, then, see you here at six." Tammy headed up the aisle.

"Hey," Denise said, "do you want to stop by early and work that scene one more time?"

Tammy smiled. "I don't think you'll need to."

Tammy and Kev left. Denise stayed seated on the front row and looked up to the stage. She wished she could be as sure as Tammy was. Perhaps it was too ambitious, writing and starring in a one-woman show. She shouldn't have let Tammy talk her out of getting another actor. But it was too late now.

It had been so easy to write the role of Beverly, but not so easy to become her. Beverly had lived in Denise's head for all the months she worked on the play, so long that she seemed real. If Denise failed to bring her emotions across, it would seem just like a betrayal.

But Denise didn't have kids. How could she know what it felt like to lose a child in a car accident? Denise had to figure out a way to get into Beverly's head, somehow, or the scene wouldn't work. Then Denise would have let the both of them down.

***

In Denise's dream, it was the night of the play, and she was on stage performing, but the house was empty. Denise kept performing, but the lights seemed brighter than usual.

A shout interrupted her performance. A booming voice from the darkened house, "Bravo! Bravo!"

Denise knew it wasn't Rich. The voice was deeper, and it almost reverberated in her head. She stepped out to edge of the stage and shielded her eyes, trying to find the source of the voice. Near the middle of the house sat a man dressed in a 19th century costume. No, not a costume; this was how the man dressed. He stood, giving Denise a wild ovation. "Bravo! Bravo!" Denise couldn't tell if the man mocked her, but he certainly frightened her.

Denise backed away toward the wings. When she turned, the man was right there in front of her, smiling. He put his hand on her shoulder, but she couldn't scream.

"Miss?" Denise's jump into consciousness startled the woman standing over her, and the woman pulled her hand back. "Sorry. You okay?"

Denise still sat in the chair where Tammy had left her. She wiped her eyes. "What time is it?"

"8:30."

"In the morning?"

"How long have you been here?" the woman asked.

"I must have fallen asleep. Sorry. I'll clear out."

"Take your time."

77

Denise rubbed her neck. "I think I've been here long enough."

***

Denise finished her makeup and checked her costume. Kev poked his head into the dressing room. He served double duty as lighting director and stage manager. "Five minutes."

"Thank you, five minutes. How's the crowd?"

"The house is almost a quarter full, and we still have people coming in."

"Good. I'll be up in a minute."

"Break a leg," Kev said.

"Thanks."

Denise checked her makeup once more, then headed to the stage. She was as ready as she'd ever be, but she still hadn't figured out how to get into Beverly's head, and she knew it.

Denise took her place onstage and nodded to Kev. The crowd noises faded as the house light dimmed. The music cued, the curtains opened, and Denise was on.

The costume changes went smoother than she thought they would. The audience seemed to be enjoying the show, and even laughed in the right places. During her "Shelly the High School Girl" monologue, she dropped a couple of lines, but she didn't let that fluster her. She headed offstage at blackout for the final costume change.

Denise yanked off the cheerleading sweater and pulled on an apron. She tied a kerchief to her head, and then took her place. Kev hit the lights.

Denise stood center stage, in a single spotlight. "My husband doesn't understand why I refuse to say our little girl is gone," she said.

As Beverly, Denise told the story of the day her daughter Faith ran out into the street and died when a car ran over her. She fought the urge to put more sadness into her voice. Just say the words, Tammy had told her. Be in the moment.

"I don't know," Denise said, "if Bill believes in God anymore. I can't blame him if he doesn't. I sometimes wonder if he's angry with me because I do. I hear him at night, in our bed, talking in the darkness. He asks God why He took our child from us. Bill's so angry, so hurt. He doesn't under-

78

stand that our child is still here."

Denise gathered herself together, tried to put herself more into the moment. She looked out into the crowd. Then, up in the balcony, she saw a little girl.

The girl stood with her hands on the front rail. She wore a simple dress, and her hair fell over her face. She watched Denise with bright eyes.

Molly Welch. She died of pneumonia. Only eight years old.

"I know I can't hold her anymore," Denise said, "or hear her voice, or see her grow. But she's with me, no matter how far away she is. That's how far a mother's love goes."

The words flowed from her, practiced script, but Denise never looked away from the little girl.

"Do you know how much Mama loves you? How it hurts so much that you're gone? Of course you do, because you're not really gone. You know because you can hear me. You can see me. Even now, you see me, and you hear me. I know you do, because I see you too. I feel you. Even now."

The little girl in the balcony smiled, and placed her hands to her chest. Tears trickled down her cheeks.

"You will never be dead to me. You will never be a memory. I love you too much to let that happen. I will always have my Faith."

With the final line, the stage lights went down. When they came back up, the audience applauded and stood to their feet in ovation. Denise bowed, accepted their applause, and then left the stage as the curtains closed.

Denise was taking off her apron in the dressing room when Tammy came in. She hugged Denise. "Oh, honey, that was incredible! Look at my arms. I still have goose bumps. What a show! That last scene really came together. And you thought you wouldn't figure out how to play that last scene."

"I almost didn't. But it came to me onstage. I spent so much time trying to get into Beverly's head, I forgot she wouldn't be there. She wouldn't be thinking about herself. Only her daughter."

"I am so proud of you. The way you looked up, as if you were talking to your daughter in Heaven, well, it just blew me away. It was so powerful. You found your moment. No hysterics, just one single tear."

"What? I didn't know I cried up there." Denise looked in the mirror.

On her cheek, she saw in the makeup the path of the single tear. She felt another coming.

"See?" Tammy said. "That's what I'm talking about. That's living in the moment. You put an angel in the balcony, and just talked to her."

"I didn't have to," Denise said. "There was one there already."

Andi

Mary SanGiovanni

Mary SanGiovanni is the author of Bram Stoker-nominated novel *The Hollower* and its forthcoming sequel *Found You* from Leisure Books. Her short story collection, *Under Cover of Night*, was published in 2002, and her short fiction has appeared in a number of periodicals in print and online, as well as anthologies. She is also co-editor of the forthcoming GSHW anthology *Dark Territories*. Visit Mary online at www.MarySanGiovanni.com.

Inside Spencer State Hospital, where the moonlight flickered through the filmy cataracts of glass and the shadows scuttled and gathered across fading floors, the dry throaty hallways whispered, "Help me . . . Help me . . ." The mice and the insects turned away. The building creaked, waiting, and the voices in the floor answered, "Where are you? Just tell me where you are."

***

The first time Andi disappeared had been five months ago. Just after the accident, Ryan Carter knew, she'd been traumatized; she had shivered and huddled against the hospital mattress when he tried to stroke her cheek. Over time, she got better and came home. That Saturday night when she disappeared, she'd looked so beautiful, just like she used to. Her eyes gazed at him with clear love and recognition. She'd been wearing clean jeans that still hung a little off her narrow hips. Her hair had been washed, a blonde pulled back into a neat ponytail. And she'd been smiling, doggonit, for the first time in five months. Smiling at him.

***

She was gone for six days.

He'd carried the cell phone everywhere, checking it for the little envelope icon that indicated a text message, the little phone receiver icon that meant a voicemail message or a missed call. He kept the phone on his desk when he worked. On the night table when he slept. In his pocket when he was out. It was almost never more than a foot away from him, and he stole glances at it periodically, checking the time, making some excuse even to himself to pick it up, to count minutes and then time markers for how long he'd give her before he really got mad, before he called the police, before he'd even consider the possibility that she walked out on him.

He called the police early the following morning, as soon as his sleepless eyes could discern a time on the digital clock that seemed reasonable to call. They asked a lot of questions and told him all kinds of facts about missing people that he didn't really hear. They didn't find her.

Instead, she returned on her own that following Thursday evening—walked right in the door. Ryan had tried to talk to her, laughing and crying, wanting to yell at her for worrying him for six days. Andi just stood there and let herself be manipulated by his embraces, molded into a hug. He kissed unresponsive lips, as if the whole act was completely foreign to her, and she seemed at an utter loss for answers to his questions. In fact, the only time she looked at him, it chilled his heart. Dark, haunted, tired eyes gazed from a pale, frightened face, trying to place him. She said nothing. She went upstairs and locked herself in the bathroom. Fifteen minutes later, he heard the water through the pipes and figured she was taking a bath. When she came out, she fell into his arms and cried. Her look told him she knew him again. A stream of sounds from her lips, muffled into his chest, made no coherent words but the tone of them suggested apology, and fear. He'd only caught one word: Spencer.

She couldn't tell him where she'd been—couldn't remember what she'd done or how she'd gotten all the way down Route 95 just over the Delaware-New Jersey border, but then she'd remembered, in bits and floating pieces, flashes of face or rooms. She'd driven the better part of the night to get home, or what she thought, somewhere in the instinct part of her brain, might be home.

Doctors called it dissociative fugue, and offered the opinion that it had been brought on by the accident. They said such fugues could last days, months, even years. Sometimes the sufferer never fully remembered who he or she had been, and started over with a different life in a different place altogether. Some people who were missing who were never found were just such people.

The thought that Andi could do that, that some part of her brain could shut out all memory of him and his life with her, absolutely terrified him.

***

There were other times. He thought it would get easier, the waiting and the worrying. He thought that eventually, he'd be able to sleep, secure in the assumption that, like always, she'd come back eventually. Sometimes it was three days, sometimes, two. Once it took her fifteen days to remember.

A good husband, he thought, would insist she keep the therapy appointments. A good husband would, in fact, take her there and bring her home. A good husband would find ways to watch over her until the fugue states stopped. And Ryan wanted to be a good husband. But she didn't want to face the accident, didn't want to deconstruct and rebuild and explore foundations. It reminded her of the hospital she'd been to as a teenager. She grew more despondent and more resentful and Ryan began to doubt what, exactly, a good husband should do in his wife's case. In the end, he decided that maybe when good husbands did bad things—like causing accidents—the best way to make up for it was to do what made his wife happy.

Besides, the doctors said the fugues would go away, eventually.

He hoped they'd go away for good, before Andi did.

***

"Help me . . ."

Last night she finally called. The message that came from Ryan's voicemail sounded different than the times before. It was lonely and small and weak, unable to stand on its own against the big empty silence engulfing his living room. When Andi called, she always sounded confused, but not . . . gone, not like that—

"Help me, Ryan . . ."

—like the way voices might sound from the particular end of very long tunnels that didn't lay in this world anymore.

83

Ryan frowned and spoke to the machine, a fresh kind of panic lacing into his voice, panic like the first time she'd done this, the first time she'd called.

"Where are you this time, baby?" he asked as if she could hear him.

Her next words, which gave him the eerie impression of a direct answer, sounded stronger than anything she'd said yet, a tinge of eager impatience lacing their edges. "I'm in a hospital. No, I'm not hurt, not a hospital like that. No doctors here, or patients anymore. An old place, full of shushing and whispering and memories. The floors talk and the hallways sigh past me. I don't remember this place. Please. Please come get me. I can't remember the car. Where it is, what kind, or even if I had a car. I don't think I remember your face." Here, she sounded very close to tears. "I had this number and your name written down in my purse, and your voice sounds kind, and I remember Ryan, Ryan, the name makes me smile and feel warm, and I'm scared here and cold, and I need you, I'm sure I do. I need you to come get me, to get me out of here, to find me and bring me home. Wherever home is. I trust you, but I can't remember why. The sign outside says Spencer. It's a hospital."

The click that followed left him cold and breathless.

He did some Internet searches on the information she gave him and found a Spencer State Hospital in Roane County, West Virginia. "How'd she get all the way down to West Virginia?" He printed what he could find, including directions. He threw some clothes and a toothbrush into a suitcase, grabbed his wallet and keys, and left. It was at least a seven-hour drive, Route 95 over the New Jersey-Delaware border, and he wanted to be there before the light of dawn gave her any idea of wandering out and away again, into an even darker mist of obscurity.

***

There are places all over the earth where the air is different. Andi might have said those places were soaked through with magic, with death, with that which bleeds into this world from the other side. It gets into the ground, the clothes, the hair, the fabric of everyday life, a thick smoke, a cloying sensation of otherness, of being watched, of being waited for.

Spencer State Hospital, an old matron decaying on its weathered frame, struck Ryan as such a place. The austere cluster of buildings ate up the green sprawling plot of West Virginia land and towered over the trees, pressing against even darker hills beyond them. The unforgiving brick made Ryan ill at ease.

"An old place, full of shushing and whispering and memories. The floors talk and the hallways sigh past me. I don't remember this place."

Something else that emanated from the building, a sick-sweet perfume, a funereal floral thing that lingered in the lungs and thus turned the stomach at its edges.

Andi was born in West Virginia and raised there until she was twelve. She loved it, talked about the mountains and the mines and the farms with tenderness. She had been in a hospital once, she told him. Depression or something like that. A tendency to sleepwalk, or take off and worry her parents sick. She stayed at a place where they treated teenagers, until it had been closed down. She'd once called it a place with doctors practicing questionable ethics, a place where secrets were shushed in the hallways, and then she'd say no more about it. He'd figured on teenaged melodrama at the time, but the Internet said differently. He'd found articles of doctors mistreating patients, of disposing of the dead beneath the floors of actively used rooms, of hallways laden with pain and grief, of old ghosts that lingered in long-forgotten passages of a building holding in all the sorrow it had seen.

He could feel it in this hospital, that sense of wrongness, that utter hopelessness against forces both internal and external that wielded terrible power and absolute control. He hated it instantly. The land. The air. The building. The stuff that's gotten into the building. That's what I don't like.

That Andi had ever been in such a place—that he didn't like.

He stood inside the front hallway of the lower level and looked around. He could see little, but he heard things—bumps and groans and metallic clinks of pipes and mournful sounds that could have almost passed for voices. He started forward, unsure where she might be. Wavering a moment, he chose a hallway to a left with a sign, "Women's Ward," and made his way down. He peeked into the rooms where the doors were opened, tried a few knobs of closed doors, and found nothing but empty rooms, hollow shells with dirt floors and cracked walls and the heavy, stuffy air that gave him a cloying sense of pain and confusion.

He couldn't imagine his sweet fragile Andi spending her delicate childhood here.

Moonlight streamed jagged and haphazard through the window onto the broken tile, the graffitied walls, the peeling paint, the silhouette shambling down a crossway at the far end of the hall.

He frowned. Blinked. Counted his thudding heartbeats. "Andi?" His voice seemed small, washed over by the gloom. He trotted in the direction of the figure, hoping.

Peering in either direction, he saw nothing. A metallic clink from behind startled him, triggering his heart. He turned slowly. At first, he could hear no sound other than his own shallow breaths. Then, almost as if the volume of an old radio was being turned slowly up, he heard the crying. Long moans, heartbreaking in their utter despair, emanated from one of the empty rooms. He headed back down to the room. At its threshold, he paused, gathering up his courage in a breath, and peered in.

No one was there. He turned and found the dead woman inches from his face, dirt in her eyes, her blond hair, tumbling from her gaping mouth in maggoty clumps.

He screamed, stumbling backward, catching onto the doorframe to right himself.

She was gone, but she'd looked so much like—

Ryan shook his head, brushed himself off, and moved on. Counted his heartbeats until they returned. He wouldn't leave. Not without her. Wouldn't. Let this place turn loose all its old hurts. He had old hurts of his own on his mind.

A hot gust of air, like a breath, blew across the back of his neck and he jumped. In the next moment it felt cold, drawing the hairs there to stand on end. He was afraid to turn around, to see the dead woman who looked like Andi, to watch the dirt tumble from her mouth to the ground around his shoes. He kept walking. Footsteps seemed to echo first behind, then ahead of him, as if someone had overtaken him, and awaited him further on down the hall.

Then he noticed a small nameplate outside one of the doors. He squinted at it, surprised he'd missed it. Then he'd realized that was because it hadn't been there when he'd passed before. He would have noticed his wife's name, even under her maiden name of SHIPPLEY, ANDREA.

He walked into the room. Immediately, it felt cold. He stumbled over something and looked down. Ryan's eyes grew wide, his mouth slipping open in shock and disgust.

There were faces, some pale, some nearly blue, others a ruddy, rotting color, that gazed up from the dirt in the floor. They were buried all around so that even ears were covered; just the faces themselves, like flowers in a garden, sprouted from the dirt, disembodied. They were laid out irregularly, face-up, so to speak, so that the eyes glared first at the ceiling, then turned in unison to look at Ryan.

He choked back the solid lump that was either a scream or a bout of nausea in his throat.

"What do you want from me?" he whispered to them, and the mouths opened.

"Help me . . . Help me . . . ."

He thought he understood. "Where is she? Please, tell me where she is."

"Ryan, we'll have to stop soon," some of the mouths said, and most of them sounded like Andi, although some sounded exactly like the voice that had left him the voicemail. "I should change Lily before she gets too comfy back there. I—"

"Stop."

"Slow down, Ry. You shouldn't be driving so fa—"

"Stop!" Ryan's eyes watered, and that lump felt larger than ever, blocking off the air.

"RRRyRyRyananan," the voices echoed, out of sync. "Lololookkk outoutout!"

He hadn't meant for her to lose the baby so soon after bringing her into the world. He'd known how much Andi wanted little Lily, how much she'd needed her, how everything in Andi's life had revolved around babies and ovulation and conception and vitamins and week-markers and breasts and bottles and Pampers versus Huggies. He hadn't crashed the car on purpose, and darn it, weren't those car seats meant to protect babies? He'd put it in himself, secured it with the seatbelt, just like the directions said. He thought—he was nearly sure, in fact—that he had followed them and the accompanying picture exactly.

He hadn't done anything wrong, darn it. He hadn't been drunk, he hadn't been sleepy, he didn't even think his mind had wandered too far.

But there had been thoughts ever since Lily had been born, little thoughts in the smallest of internal voices, thoughts nearly drowned out by the patter of the rain. Sometimes, he thought in the smallest of internal voices, where thoughts weren't big enough or weighty enough to be wishes, or the stuff of heavy consciences. Worry. Doubt. Fear. Jealousy. Inferiority. The smallest of these collected heavily in his right foot and settled into the frown of his brow and mouth.

But he'd been watching the road. He thought he had. The deer had bounded suddenly onto the road and he'd swerved. Even at that speed, they should have been okay. They should have. But sometimes even good husbands crash a car just so, and little necks snap from impact and good, sleeping wives get smacked and cut by windshields and dashboards and biting seatbelts. It had been an accident.

Sometimes he thought that the death of a loved one was hard, but it was concrete, and it was final. There was closure in death. But when someone went missing . . . the endless hours of helplessness, of waiting, of turning over all the most vile, most too-awful-to-think scenarios in his mind—that was the stuff of torture. That was worse than dealing with her death, because so much mystery made the torment last indefinitely. Sometimes, he thought in that small voice, that her death would be easier to handle than her being missing. Would be better.

Good husbands were allowed that, he thought—peace and closure. Bad husbands who killed their families deserved to worry.

The faces murmured, "Nonononononono. . ." It was frustration. There had been many, he could see, with pain, with the desire to forget, or to remember, or to have strong, unfailing minds. Many who had given control over to people who had let them die, and then buried all memory of them, all trace of their deaths and so, or their lives, deep in well-treaded common ground. Many of them who found a kindred spirit in Andi, and a chance to make Ryan understand what they wanted for her, and for themselves.

They wanted to move on, to places unknown to the living likes of him. And they wanted that to be closure enough.

He hadn't meant for anything bad to ever happen to Andi. He loved her with a fierce, aching kind of love, a desperate kind. A kind that refused to accept that she wasn't ever coming back from wherever she'd gone without some proof.

The faces in the floor cried silently, and their tears, tinged with blood, streaked through the grime of their faces and turned the dirt around them dark.

They weren't sad tears, but tears of relief. Now he knew. He understood. He remembered, not doctors and fugue states and the clean hair and her smile, but funerals and arrangements and flowers that lingered in the lungs and thus turned the stomach at its edges.

Satisfied, he nodded at the faces, and they sank softly into the ground, the dirt rising up to cover them completely. His footsteps echoed in the silent hall. The moonlight fell on the front lawn, illuminating.

Ryan got into his car and started the long drive back to New Jersey.

The Man in Ragged Blue

Rob Darnell

Rob Darnell is a tree farmer. He lives in Lapeer, Michigan, and enjoys nature, reading, and operating chainsaws. His blog is his hobby; he is also fond of taking pictures of whatever strikes his fancy. He loves baseball and roots for the Detroit Tigers. Visit him online at www.robdarnell.com

The bedside clock said 3:31, but Jake was not in bed. He stood at the window, carefully peeling back the drapes.

Quincy Street was lively in the harsh February wind. Lamps lining the road provided the light necessary for him to spot his nightly caller.

Jake was still new in town. He had relocated to Parkersburg, West Virginia, from Michigan only three weeks ago. The house he rented was nice enough, and his neighbors seemed like decent people, except one of them.

He glimpsed movement at the corner. Something small and at ground level shifted and then rolled.

It turned out to be a newspaper.

He sighed and let the drapes fall back in place.

Every night since he moved in, he was awakened around this time by someone banging on his front door. Every night he would get up and look out the window, but whoever it was had fled.

The need for sleep was strong; he would have to be at work in four hours, but he was going to be the cranky guy in the office today.

He walked from the bedroom and made his way down the narrow hallway to the living room. The floorboards of the old house creaked underfoot as he crossed the living room to the picture window next to the door and peeked through the drapes.

His front yard had not been invaded.

Not yet, but any minute now and he would know which of his neighbors had taken it unto themselves to drive him out of town.

He waited patiently for what seemed like a lifetime, but the only activity outside the house was the trees rocking in the wind. Had his nightly caller seen him peeking out the window and decided to call off the commando operation?

Jake yawned. He wanted to go to bed. The weariness weighed on his eyelids and he didn't think he would last much longer.

He moved to the recliner across the room, sat down and pulled the lever to raise the footrest. He watched the minutes tick by on the wall hanging clock and tried to keep his eyes open.

He was jarred awake by someone banging on the front door.

He climbed from the chair and hurried to the window. The person outside hammered on the door several more times. Jake pulled back the drapes and looked out at his front porch.

There was a man. Heavily bearded and a little underdressed for the cold winter night. The man wore a faded blue coat, which hung unbuttoned and exposed a hairy chest and red stained bandages over his left ribcage. He also wore torn blue pants.

The man was leaning against the doorframe like he depended on it for support. Jake figured him for a local drunk. That would explain a lot. Bars back in Michigan usually ran off their customers around two in the morning, probably was the same here.

The man outside was likely confused after a long night of drinking, perhaps he was looking for the previous resident of the house. Jake remembered his landlord had mentioned something about the previous tenant being an alcoholic. Perhaps the two had been drinking buddies.

He went to the door and yanked it open.

The man who stared back at him was not drunk. Jake didn't think so because there was no scent of alcohol on him. But the man's eyes were wide and glossy, like a deer in headlights.

Jake offered, "Can I help you?"

The man looked at him a minute. He started to speak, but then collapsed to the porch.

Jake felt his heart skip. He hesitated long enough to think about what had just happened and then rolled the man over onto his back. He held a hand over the man's nose and mouth but didn't feel a breath.

Another moment of hesitation and he was hurrying back through the house. He scooped the phone off the kitchen wall and started to call for an ambulance when he glanced toward the front door and saw the man was no longer there.

He put the phone back in its cradle and crossed to the front door.

The man was gone. Jake looked to either side of the porch, the man had not rolled off, nor were there tracks in the snow to follow. He stepped outside just to be sure. There was nothing to see, but when he turned to go back inside he heard a sound like someone moaning.

"Hello?" he said, not loudly for he had no desire to wake his neighbors. There was no answer. After a moment of silence he went back inside and closed the door.

He was up at 7:15 and made it to work on time, though his day was not very productive. He sat at his desk, answered the phone when it rang, but did little else. He was thankful when the day ended and he could head home.

When he pulled in the driveway, his next-door-neighbor was salting the sidewalk leading up to Jake's front door. Jake had spoken with Andy a few times, he was a friendly old man and very informative.

Jake climbed from the car and advanced the sidewalk to greet Andy at the foot of the porch.

"Hello." Andy lowered his snow shovel and offered a hand, which Jake readily grasped. "How have you been?"

"I've been better," Jake admitted and stifled a yawn. "I haven't been sleeping well."

"Oh?"

"Yeah, ever since I moved in someone wakes me up at three in the morning, banging on my door. Do you know anything about it?"

Andy looked thoughtful a moment, and then nodded. "I might. You never saw who it was?"

"Last night, I did. I think." He pondered, unsure how to go on, and then just decided to tell it all.

Andy listened without interrupting. Jake told him about last night, how he'd seen the man and how the man had disappeared when he went to call an ambulance. He finished the story with the moaning he'd heard when he stepped out on the porch.

"Yeah," Andy said, bobbing his head.

Jake was pondering whether to take that as an insult when Andy said more.

"You'll have to get used to it, Jake."

"Get used to it?"

"This is Quincy Hill." Andy pointed across the street where the top of the hill could be seen behind the house there.

Andy went on: "During the Civil War, there was a tent city up there where sick and wounded men were hospitalized. But conditions in the tent city were so bad that some of the men crawled down the hill and tried to find their way to the hospital in town. Most of them died."

Jake stared at him a moment, and then said, "You're not serious."

"Not everyone believes it," Andy said. "But some of us in the neighborhood have heard the moaning."

"Has anyone actually seen the ghosts?"

"Not that I know of, besides you."

Jake didn't know what to think, he had never been one to believe ghost stories. Maybe Andy was a little off his rocker, Jake barely knew the guy.

"Your house is pretty old," Andy said. "My guess is it was here back before the Civil War. Your ghost must have found the place and in a fit of desperation, he tried to wake someone to help him and died."

Jake shrugged. "Maybe."

"But don't worry about it," Andy said. He slashed his shovel into the bucket of salt nearby and proceeded to sprinkle the salt over Jake's sidewalk. "You'll get used to it."

Jake thanked him and went inside.

***

That night he stayed up, not by choice this time, but because he was unable to sleep. He didn't know if Quincy Hill was really haunted by the spirits of Civil War soldiers, but he did know a man mysteriously disappeared from his front porch.

He sat in the recliner and watched the clock on the wall. At fifteen minutes to four the familiar banging had returned to his door.

This time Jake was prepared. He jumped from the recliner, crossed the room and flung the door open.

It was the same man from last night, in the blue coat and pants, and the bandages over his ribcage had not been changed.

Jake felt goosebumps breakout on his arms.

"Will you help me, sir?" the man said, he spoke with an accent that Jake recognized from a vacation to Ireland years ago. The man started to say more, but the words seemed to have caught in his throat, and then he dropped to his knees and fell forward.

Jake caught him halfway to the floor. He managed to lift the man back to his feet and help him into the house.

"Do you have whiskey?" the man said in a voice barely audible as Jake lowered him into the recliner.

Fortunately Jake had kept a stocked liquor cabinet for years. He stepped to it and retrieved a bottle of Jack Daniel. He unscrewed the cap and helped the man hold it to drink.

The man had three long swallows. He smiled a little, and then closed his eyes. His hand fell away from the bottle and landed on his knee. He did not move again.

Jake took the bottle away and stepped into the kitchen where he drained it in the sink. When he returned to the living room the man was gone.

There was no disturbance the next night. There were no more disturbances for the two years that Jake lived in the house on Quincy Street, and he knew the soldier had found rest.

For Just One Night

Nate Southard

Nate Southard is the author of the novella *Just Like Hell* and the graphic novels *Drive* and *A Trip to Rundberg*. His first novel will see print in 2009. He lives in Austin, Texas, with his girlfriend. You can learn more fascinating tidbits at www.natesouthard.com or myspace.com/natesouthard.

"I'm cold."

"I know." Jamie placed her hand on top of her brother's. She wanted to do more, but fear stopped her. Patrick's bones felt like twigs under the parchment of his skin, brittle dead things that could snap at the slightest pressure. Instead, she gave the hand a light pat and wished she could do more.

"Are you cold?"

"A little."

The April air still held some of winter's chill, but the first signs of spring had arrived. Even so, it was almost midnight, and a breeze cut across Ram Stadium's home bleachers. Jamie shivered and pressed her arms hard against her sides. She looked at her brother—bundled in heavy coat, scarf, and wool cap—and hated herself for not being able to hold him close. "We can leave if you want," she said, hoping he would accept the offer.

Instead, Patrick shook his head, his eyes never leaving the grass of Shepherd College's football field. "I'm okay. We don't have much longer to wait, and I really want to see her. Don't you?"

"Yeah." A lie. They were sitting in the night air because Patrick wanted to. It had been his idea from the beginning, and she'd never found a good reason to tell him no. She'd searched long and hard for a reason, but he was too excited about it to be denied.

He shivered beside her and let out a shuddering breath. A groan escaped him.

"You okay?" she asked.

"Hurts again. I'm okay."

"Patrick, are you sure?"

"Yes. I'll just have to take a dose when we get home."

Take a dose. That meant she'd have to stick a needle in his arm again. Patrick's battle with cancer had been a tough one, full of remissions and returns, painful symptoms and even more painful treatments, too much suffering for a boy of barely twenty. Once the doctors handed down their final verdict of terminal, she'd gone out and bought Patrick his first hit of heroin. If her brother was going to die, he wasn't going to die in pain.

The opiate had taken his agony away in a single moment. He'd smiled for the first time in months as his head lolled back and his eyes drooped shut. Then he'd laughed. It was almost a happy sound, something between the cackle of a clown and the wail of a ghost, but it had been laughter. From that day on, she'd dosed Patrick every time he asked. She didn't kid herself about him becoming an addict. Just another disease he wouldn't live long enough to defeat.

She checked her watch. Two 'til. "Almost there."

"I know," Patrick answered.

"You really think she'll show?"

"Of course." He sounded more than a little offended at her doubt. He shivered again, his entire body bouncing.

"We should have tried to get into Gardiner Hall. It would be warmer there."

He turned then, his blue eyes shining deep within the shadows of his gaunt face. "They wouldn't have let us in Gardiner."

"They might have.

"No. Even if they did, they wouldn't let me hang out in the women's bathroom just hoping she'll appear. This is better. This has a date, a time. We can't miss."

"But you're—"

"I'll be fine, Jamie. It's just another minute or two."

She checked her watch again. "Should be right now. It's midnight." She looked to the grassy field. Dark and emptiness and clipped green blades. Nothing more. The girl wasn't there, wasn't coming. Patrick had sat in the chill for nothing. At least she could get him inside now, take him back to her apartment where she could cook him up a batch and take his pain away for a little while. "We should go."

"Your watch is fast."

"It's not, Patrick. Let's get you out of the cold."

"Ten more minutes. If she doesn't show, we'll leave. I promise, okay?"

She looked into her brother's eyes, once full of life and warmth but now a haven of pain, weakness, and addiction. Even now, however, there was still some of the old Patrick in them, a tiny spark that was still her brother. She wondered how long that spark might last. Another month? A week?

"Okay. Five minutes, then we go."

"Deal."

She gave him a smile, but he looked away, his eyes darting to the field.

"Wow." His voice was barely more than a breath, but it carried more awe than Jamie had ever heard.

She turned to follow his eyes. She didn't want to look away from her brother, but she knew she had to. She'd promised Patrick, and she intended to enjoy this little dose of magic with him. Her eyes came to rest on the end zone right in front of the Boone Field House, and her breath caught in her throat.

The girl was real.

She walked right through the goalpost, flickering like a bad television picture. She wore a beautiful green dress, the sash across her chest white and crisp. Auburn hair hung long and straight, almost concealing the bleeding wound at her temple.

The girl smiled, a picture of perfect happiness.

Jamie let out a small gasp. "Oh my God."

"She's beautiful," Patrick said as if agreeing with her.

The girl continued her walk. Slow but confident steps carried her across the field. She reached the ten-yard line and flickered again, dropping out of the world before reappearing at the fifteen. Her smile never wavered. Her chin remained high and proud, her eyes on the goalpost at the field's opposite end. If she noticed the siblings watching her, she didn't show it.

Jamie gave Patrick's hand the smallest squeeze possible, and even that was harder than she dared. "Why here?" she asked as the girl crossed the twenty-five.

"What do you mean?"

"You said she died in Gardiner Hall, right? She fell in the bathroom?

Why does she show up here?"

"She was a Homecoming Queen."

"So what?"

"You know why, Jamie."

"I don't. I'm sorry, but I don't. It's too easy."

Patrick sighed, his air leaving in a slow, tired breath.

"She was happy here."

Jaime tore her gaze away from the girl to give Patrick a glance. "You really think so?"

"Yeah. For just one night, maybe, but she was happy here. She was the center of everything, a Queen. Maybe the next day she had to start thinking about finals again, or how she really didn't like her major or her friends, or how life was already telling her nothing would turn out the way she wanted. For one night that didn't matter, though."

The girl reached the fifty. She shimmered under the moon, her image crackling at the edges, wandering in and out of focus like old newsreel footage. Her smile beamed, and Jamie could see light glint off the blood that coated her wound.

Patrick breathed again. It sounded wet, labored. When he swallowed, it echoed through the stadium. "For just one night, that girl was royalty. She didn't have a care in the world. Who wouldn't want to go back to that?"

Jamie closed her eyes, imagining a time when she had felt the same way. She sensed the approach of her tears, and she willed her eyes dry. Now wasn't the time. "She is beautiful," she said.

"I know." His voice was a whisper, almost nothing.

Jamie watched in silence as the girl continued her march across the field. The green dress swished over the grass without sound. The night fell quiet as sadness as the Homecoming Queen entered the opposing end zone and disappeared, gone until the following April.

Jamie watched the field for a long time. She wished she could make the same walk and then she cast the thought aside. Patrick needed her, and she would take care of him until the end. Maybe then she could think about walking with her head held high. Maybe she could think about that smile. That was later, though. Right now she had to get Patrick warm and numb.

"C'mon, baby brother. Let's go."

She stood, her knees popping, and only then did she realize Patrick had fallen silent. She turned to look down at her brother and found him slumped forward, still.

"Patrick?"

No answer. He didn't move, didn't speak.

"Patrick?" She sat down beside him again and nudged his shoulder. His body moved a little, but he didn't respond.

Jamie sighed. She wanted to say something, but nothing felt right. Nothing worked. Instead, she wrapped both arms around her brother and held him tight. For just one night, it felt good.

Acknowledgements

— I have to first say thank you to the writers, who did a great job in keeping with the same tone and style as the first edition. The level of quality and professionalism each of you maintain made this anthology the best it could be.

— I want to thank Keith, Cheryl, and the staff at Woodland Press for allowing me to have so much fun with a project that is so dear to my heart. Also, I want to thank you for your dedication to quality and honesty.

— A special thank you is in order for our esteemed Governor, Joe Manchin, III, for the support and encouragement for arts and literature in our great state. Your foreword for this project is appreciated and your eagerness to show your blessing is treasured.

— Thanks to Joe R. Lansdale for the kind (and very cool) words. Your talent amazes me, but your kindness is unmatched. Thank you for taking the time from your busy schedule to read and comment.

— Thank you is hardly enough when it comes to the gratitude I have for my wife, Jewell, who allows me to spend many hours working on these projects. If I ever had a fan, I know it is you. I love you more than you will ever know.

Michael Knost is an author, editor, and publisher of dark and speculative fiction and resides in Logan, West Virginia. He has written several books, tons of short stories, and many nonfiction pieces.

What Others Are Saying

As a collection, the thirteen stories in *Legends of the Mountain State 2: More Ghostly Tales from the State of West Virginia* work cohesively to paint a multi-layered portrait of a working-class region overflowing with superstition and ghostly lore. As in the first volume, editor Knost does a commendable job balancing the terror and tenderness.

— Vince A. Liaguno, *Dark Scribe Magazine*

What an assemblage of writers! And, in closing, a few words to the editor (I wonder if Knost rhymes with Ghost; it really should!)

— David M. Kinchen, *Huntingtonnews.net*

Hardboiled, Southern Gothic. I loved it. It's lean and mean and it doesn't care if you like it, which is what makes me like it all the better. Written with a razor on the back of a dead bloated redneck cracker down by the river side, the mountains in view, this is one excellent read.

— Joe R. Lansdale

Legends of the Mountain State remains our number one local title. This chilling anthology has captured the imagination of many Mountain State readers, as well as travelers from across the country.

— Lill Neace, *Borders, West Virginia*

Legends of the Mountain State is one of those rare books that brings someone my age (my mid-forties) back to my childhood. It conjures up memories of how I'd lie beneath the covers at night with a flashlight, reading scary stories long after I was supposed to be asleep. It returns me to those days when my friends and I would sit outside at night, maybe by a campfire, maybe just in someone's backyard, and we'd tell each other tales about men with hooks for hands, which houses in town were haunted, and how someone's big brother had a friend who once saw a big, hairy creature roaming through the woods.

— J.G. Faherty, *Fear Zone*

Legends of the Mountain State is a superior horror anthology filled with all new tales to keep the lights on at night and the out-of-state tourists away from West Virginia.

— Harriet Klausner, *Harriet Klausner's Review*

Reminiscent of a book I read as a young man, *Alfred Hitchcock's Stories to be Read with the Lights On*. That book scared me then. The dark collection of stories in *Legends* give me the creeps right now! Great story-telling!

— Alex Lockett

APPALACHIAN AUTHORS.
APPALACHIAN STORIES.
APPALACHIAN PRIDE.

Woodland Press

Also publishers of other great titles under these imprints
World Literary Services
LNAB

RESELLERS / BOOKSTORES:
Stock Woodland Press Titles
By Contacting

Woodland Press, LLC

118 Woodland Drive
CHAPMANVILLE, WV 25508
Email:
woodlandpressllc@mac.com
Telephone (304) 752-7152
FAX (304) 752-9002
www.woodlandpress.com

- or -

West Virginia Book Company

1125 Central Avenue,
Charleston WV 25302
Telephone 304-342-1848
FAX: (304) 343-0594
Toll Free: 1-888-982-7472
www.wvbookco.com

Deep into that darkness peering,
long I stood there, wondering,
fearing, doubting, dreaming
dreams no mortal ever dared to
dream before.

— Edgar Allen Poe

Woodland Press, LLC

www.woodlandpress.com

Paperback, 204 pages
Author F. Keith Davis

THIS YEAR'S MOST SHOCKING STORY— It's been called West Virginia's barbaric version of the Black Dahlia murder. Seventy-six years ago, in the cradle of southern West Virginia's most rugged mountain range, a bizarre murder grabbed national headlines, mostly due to the peculiar circumstances surrounding the gruesome homicide. Now, a book—a new revision offering greater detail and newly discovered information—takes another look at this puzzling account. A true crime drama, it features a number of white-collar suspects, an intense community scandal and a shocking gangland-style execution that still baffles law enforcement. This expanded edition offers lots of new information. The unexpected ghostly manifestations and the haunted rumors that have occurred since the murder are also discussed in this award-winning project—published by Quarrier Press and Woodland Press, LLC. **$15.95**

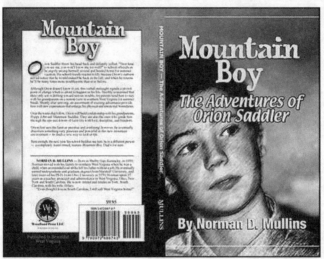

MOUNTAIN BOY: The Adventures of Orion Saddler — Orion Saddler threw his head back and defiantly screamed, "Next time you see me, you won't know me too well!" to school officials as he angrily swung himself around and headed home for summer vacation. Over the weeks to follow, Orion will build a strong relationships with his grandparents, Poppy John and Mammaw Saddler. *Mountain Boy: The Adventures of Orion Saddler* is an inspiring book that will be a wonderful edition for your personal library. **$9.95**

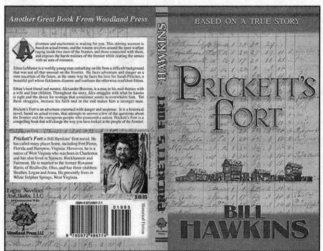

PRICKETT'S FORT — Prickett's Fort is a rich adventure crammed with danger and suspense. It is a romance that exposes the innocence and intensity of a first love. It is a historical novel, based on actual events, that attempts to answer a few of the questions about the frontier and the courageous people who once pioneered a nation. This volume is inspiring and powerful. **$19.95**

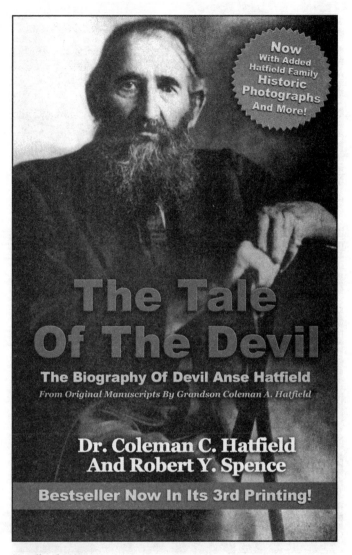

Now With Added Hatfield Family Historic Photographs And More!

The Tale Of The Devil

The Biography Of Devil Anse Hatfield

From Original Manuscripts By Grandson Coleman A. Hatfield

Dr. Coleman C. Hatfield And Robert Y. Spence

Bestseller Now In Its 3rd Printing!

Hardback, 328 pages

A BESTSELLER — *Tale of the Devil* is the powerful story of the legendary Anderson "Devil Anse" Hatfield, of feud fame, beginning with his childhood in frontier Appalachia. The story also covers his Civil War days as a noted Confederate soldier, a determined feudist and his final years after the vendetta ended, giving a richly detailed background into just who this man was and from where he came. This handsome hardbound edition gives readers a captivating and enlightening bird's-eye view of the Hatfield-McCoy feud, the killings, and the post-feud years when the shooting subsided. Through this effort, Dr. Hatfield received the prestigious "Tamarack Author of the Year" award in 2004.   **$18.95**

Softcover, 612 pages

This is the authorized story of West Virginia Governor Arch A. Moore, Jr. Inside this work, numerous stories include the near-fatal wounding of Sgt. Moore by a German machine gun in World War II; a gerrymandered Congressional race in which the entire Democratic Establishment, including three Presidents, tried to defeat him; the few minutes Moore was "premier" of the Soviet Union; being shot down in Vietnam and his 1968 helicopter crash in Lincoln County; the 1976 trial and acquittal. It is a an exceptionally researched and executed literary work, authored by former WV Tax Commissioner Brad Crouser.   **$32.95**

Softcover, 192 pages

"As a scion of one of the feuding families of the Allegheny and Cumberland hills, and one whose forebearers began their trek westward from the Virginia coast, I offer the following for all who may be interested or desire to hear the facts from one who has first-hand knowledge of the people of whom he writes." —Dr. Coleman C. Hatfield

This unique book is about two proud families. It is a title that includes a comprehensive timeline of the Hatfield family migration westward and documents the history before, during and following the bloody Hatfield and McCoy feud era. This book uses a timeline format and is also a pictorial history that features rare and interesting photographs from both families.   **$18.95**

For more information about Woodland Press, LLC,
of Chapmanville, WV, write:

WOODLAND PRESS, LLC
118 Woodland Drive
Chapmanville, WV 25508
Email: woodlandpressllc@mac.com

Woodland Press, LLC